BAUBLES FROM BONES

➤ Summer 2024 ➤

Shane Gallaher · *Editor*
Elyse Leskovic · *Editor, Artist*
Joel Troutman · *Editor, Typesetter*
Caroline Ritzert · · · · · · · · · · · · · · · · · *Social Media Manager*

Illustrations: Elyse Leskovic: *(27, 46, 55, 76, 88, 130)*, Joel Troutman: *(47)*, Elyse Leskovic and Joel Troutman: *(89, 110)*

Cover art: Gabriel Stratulat

Baubles From Bones: Issue 1, Summer 2024 [ISBN 979-8-218-43405-2]. Independently published and distributed: Pittsburgh, PA. Printed in USA.

baublesfrombones.com

TABLE OF CONTENTS

⫷ FICTION ⫸

⫷ POETRY ⫸

⫷ EDITORIAL ⫸

THE FEAST OF THE CHANGES

Katherine Traylor

Red Boy had traveled with Big Beast for months, wandering from the city where he'd grown up into the wild nothing of the Other Ones. Every day they stopped in some out-of-the-way place to gather things that had no value. Every night they stopped to eat and ruminate about the day.

Big Beast ate more than Red Boy, of course. He was as big as a house when you could see him. (In the city he was less there, but to Red Boy he was always huge). But though he needed a lot of food, he always saw to it that Red Boy ate well, too. Anyway, Red Boy was learning to find what they needed.

They carried it all in big cloth sacks. The sacks grew fuller slowly. After all this time (three months, Red Boy thought), they were only a quarter full. As strong as Big Beast was, and as good at finding things, you'd think his sack would be full, but he had to eat and eat to feed his great body. **The better you eat, the better you grow,** Big Beast said once. **As you grow more, you find more, but you also eat more. So you must find more and keep less, day by day.** So even though Big Beast was very strong (he'd carried Red Boy, that night when he was sad and hurting), he usually had no more left to put in his sack after dinner than Red Boy did.

Red Boy wanted to help. He knew how much he owed his friend. But he always guessed wrong: he hadn't yet mastered the complex arithmetic of Big Beast's needs and tastes.

Big Beast assured him it was fine. **You have your own taste. You'll find what's best for you soon.** Anyway, they could leave things behind, or trade them on the rare occasions when they found Big Beast's cousins under trees by the roadside, or hiding in bus shelters, or winding through tight woods behind filling stations. Those Other Ones had their own tastes, too, and could often use what Big Beast and Red Boy could not.

Now Big Beast and Red Boy were in a landfill, which Big Beast said was one of the best places for finding things. (*Landfill.* Once Red Boy had gone to school, and that was where he'd learned the word.) It was so big it looked like a world made of garbage: every mountain a black bag, every skyscraper a soda can. The people were so small you couldn't see them: smaller than ants, unimportant in this strange, upsetting vastness.

They'd come late in the day, looking for things growing in unwatched places. The vast stinking slopes glittered in a way that would have been beautiful if the smell hadn't been so horrifying.

Shifting his furry bulk over the last rise, Big Beast sighed a groaning sigh. **We'll start here.**

When they'd first traveled together, Red Boy had thought Big Beast was patronizing him. (*Patronize.* His mother had said that to someone once. She'd been angry, unhappy. It had been raining. *Don't patronize me.*) He was little, and he didn't know what he was doing. But gradually he realized that he was helping, though he couldn't carry much. His small, sharp eyes could see into places where the Other One's huge black ones couldn't look. His fingers were quick and slender. He found things. He was useful. That was nice to be.

Of course, he didn't know what they were looking for here.

Use your eyes, Big Beast said, smiling in his way that turned his whole brown shaggy face into one joyous mask. **Look wherever you think you should look. You'll find something.**

He started looking himself, and Red Boy started looking, too. With his foot he pushed aside a few trash bags at the base of a large heap. After the first one started leaking, though, he quickly moved on to look in other places. He picked through crumbling cardboard with finicky fingers, skated through slime, scrutinized eggshells black with age and strange new life. After a while his nose grew desensitized. Soon he remembered he didn't have to stay clean, anyway. Big Beast seemed to like him no matter how he smelled.

He found a one-eyed doll, a refrigerator with a thousand beetles inside, a forest of soda straws, a thick pool of slime. Slowly he wandered away from Big Beast, over the top of the trash mountain towards nothing in particular.

He found a box inside other boxes, both wet with rotting substances that smelled quite indescribable. Under the innermost box, something caught his eye: a spot where a patch of red cellophane crossed the red logo on a shoebox, making a crimson patch much deeper and brighter than either place alone. With his new-honed eyes, he saw that this was one of the places Big Beast told him about, where the unseen grew into something that climbed beyond the human world.

"Here." He reached into the red place and closed his hand over two spheres, round and cool, about the size of golf balls. When he pulled them out, they were round red gems that sparkled like cut-glass cherries.

Big Beast came over the hill, his brown elephant legs kicking aside mountains of refuse. The familiar smell of him, a deep brown musk common to large wild things, replaced the stench of garbage. **Beautiful,** he said admiringly. **You should eat them.**

"It isn't nighttime," he said uncertainly. Usually they saved what they could for dinner, unless they found something particularly tasty.

Near enough. Shading his pumpkin-sized brow, Big Beast regarded the sinking sun. **And you are hungry. Little Beasts must take care to stay fed. Besides, you found them.**

"Here." Red Boy handed him one of the cherries. It was heavy, as if made from glass, though he knew by now it was something else. "At least have one."

Big Beast held it up to the sun, letting the light shine through it, nodding as the red light swirled starry and dark inside the center of the not-fruit. Then he handed it back. **It's yours. Red, for Red Boy.**

Red Boy was hungry enough that he didn't protest, though he knew Big Beast must be much hungrier than him. Brushing the cherries on his shirt, he bit into the first one, crushing through a surface that broke like thick hard candy. It tasted like a ghost of fruit, but also as if something were speaking to him deep within his mind.

He finished the broken sphere in three good bites. As the singing of that cherry-thing hummed deep in his mind, he ate the other. Then he dusted off his hands (not sticky, though he felt they should be) and looked at Big Beast. "What now?"

Big Beast laid his broad hand atop Red Boy's head. It was warm as an oven and gave more shade than a sun-hat. **Now we keep looking awhile for whatever we might find. When it's too dark to look, we'll go and rest.** It was what they did every night, but the repetition was comforting.

For the rest of the afternoon, they were quiet. Red Boy stayed close to Big Beast, listening to the shlush of their footsteps as they picked their way through hills of garbage. They found a few more things (a plastic cup that hummed like it had a bee inside; a blue plate smashed to pieces that stayed together in loose order wherever they were moved). Big Beast seemed happy to find them. But he was mostly quiet, perhaps thinking, and Red Boy was sleepy after his meal and wanted to go home, wherever that was tonight. "Can we camp?" he asked.

Of course, Big Beast said. So they went out through the mountains of lost things and into a glade of trees, where they made a fire together and settled themselves for the evening.

Red Boy knew he helped Big Beast with his hunting. At the same time, he knew that Big Beast did more for him than he could ever repay. His friend's constant presence was like a brown tower at the edge of his vision, a sentinel telling him he was safe to explore no matter where he went. When they slept back to back near the campfire, the warmth of the Other One's shaggy fur was as cozy as a blanket. Big Beast never spoke aloud, but there was a rumble between their minds when he talked that was almost like speech. Red Boy hadn't seen another human in months, but he didn't mind. He was never lonely, never hungry, never sad.

Long ago, he'd lived with his mother. Though she had tried, there had been things she couldn't keep pushing back. He'd often been sad, and sometimes lonely, though he'd tried not to let her know. In the end, they hadn't been able to stay together no matter how much she'd wanted to.

He thought of her sometimes, when he looked sideways at Big Beast and caught the shape of that strange, shaggy face that had never seen a human reflection in the mirror. His mother had been her own universe: brown, too, but smooth, and elegant and small. She wore red sweaters and desperate tension, always watching him from the corner of her eye as if he were some treasure she was afraid of losing. Big Beast watched him now, but without desperation. He trusted Red Boy, knowing that they were friends together and that Red Boy wouldn't leave him. (And if Red Boy did, then that would be his choice; Big Beast wouldn't stop him.)

He was tired all over from the long climb through garbage hills, but like every night he rested comfortably, pressed against the great warm hillside of Big Beast's fur. They stirred the fire, shared their treasures, and watched the moon rise as they ate: a cool white crescent, stark against the black sky. It faced right like a C.

"*A curl-up moon,*" Mother had said, pointing to the shape. "*When it goes the other way, like a D, that's a dancing moon. That's when you go out with your friends and have a good time. Curl-up moons are for staying in and cuddling and going to sleep.*"

He remembered little things like that, things she'd told him about the world. He never told them to Big Beast, though he knew it was the kind of knowledge Big Beast would have liked. Instead, they sat in silence, looking at the moon. That was what they did every night: ate their food and stared up at the dancing moons and the curl-up moons and the full moons in between, wide and gorgeous like the laughing mouth of the sky. There were also nights when the moon was hidden and the stars peeked eerily from the black. Then Red Boy kept his eyes down, watching the fire instead, how it cast golden moons on the huge, gentle eyes of his only friend.

Red Boy lay awake tonight, listening to Big Beast's creaking snores through the loose sough of the wind. He was remembering his mother. He wondered if he should look for her, someday, if he and Big Beast ever finished traveling. She probably missed him. He hoped she was all right.

He could still hear her voice in memory. *"Come back!"* she'd said when he'd run off into the night, hiding from what was coming for them. *"Come back! Come back!"* He remembered her face in flashing blue light, how she'd screamed when she was carried away. Though he'd stood alone there in the street, there'd been no one to know he was alone, or that he needed help. No one seemed to see him at all but the vast shadow watching from the corner of the street, which no one else seemed to notice.

He stared at the fire. He couldn't remember her face, just corners of it, the pain in her eyes, the thinness of her fingers. He didn't remember her name. It had fallen when he'd lost his own, forgetting there was more to him than *Red Boy* (red for the shirt he'd been wearing on the night he'd found his friend, the shirt he still wore after all these miles and garbage dumps). If he asked for her, he wouldn't know who to ask for.

He curled up in his blankets and closed his eyes, leaning back against his sleeping friend's fur. It was best not to think about it. He wouldn't know where to look, anyway. They seemed to have crossed half the world since that night. He didn't know where they were now, or who he was, but he knew he wasn't the same person she would be looking for.

Their travels were mostly solitary. Once in a long while

they met one of Big Beast's cousins. The Other Ones would converse in the soft unheard whisper of their customary speech, but Red Boy couldn't always hear them and could rarely understand. On that long-ago first night, alone in the arms of the thing that was carrying him far away from his mother and his home, he hadn't heard a word Big Beast had said. He'd sobbed broken for hours until the first tentative rumble came through his head: *Boy?* Through time, he'd come to understand Big Beasts, but he didn't have that rapport with the other Ones.

They looked nothing like Big Beast. Some were long and twisting, with many eyes dotted along what might have been necks or arms or tails. Others were hard-shelled like turtles, their armor shining like polished metal. One seemed to be a hillside dotted with flowers, but stood to become a vast four-footed creature with soft pink fur and a long grass cloak. One had been hiding in a river, and it slid out in a gray mass like slime or jelly when Big Beast called its improbable name.

None of these Other Ones took much interest in Red Boy. They seemed to see him as a sort of pet: a rat, maybe, or something less popular. Not a dog or a cat. But he was so unnerved by their strange appearances that he didn't mind being excluded. He sat in the sunlight when they talked, staring at the undersides of sunlit leaves and learning things from their rustlings, until Big Beast came to get him with a warm big-eyed smile and led him off down their continuing road.

Those meetings were few, the Other Ones being rare and solitary. Between them, the days went on as always, and Red Boy began to feel restless. Repeating each day incessantly, with only the landscape changing, wasn't the beautiful thing he'd imagined freedom was, back when he had not been free to go where he liked. Now he began to wonder why they should travel this way. Did Big Beast have any plan for his long, wandering life? Or was he content to find and eat a few treasures each day, to brush the ground of all the earth's roads with the soles of his massive feet and his long, dragging tail?

Then, when Red Boy had been traveling with his friend for almost a year, their weary feet led them one night into a valley glen.

It was such a shock that Red Boy thought he was dreaming. They'd been traveling for a long time over a vast empty plain, its grass brushed soft by wind bending under the starlit sky. Trees a little too sparse for beauty tossed their heads in the darkness. The road was moonlit (the moon was full and bright, perfect for parties), leading shallowly up to a ridge lined with trees, and by the same light Red Boy saw other roads converging on the same ridge. On those roads, dim figures shuffled—shambled—trotted—undulated towards the line of trees. As they all approached the ridge, Red Boy began to hear sounds besides crickets and the wind: music, laughter, crackling fires.

Something new was happening, something strange and dreamlike. Red Boy tried to understand where this place had come from, but he was distracted by the sight of his fellow travelers: long shadows swirling through the grass; mountainous monsters; tall, thin people with bundles on their backs and unknowable faces. Big Beast kept on walking forward, one step at a time, and Red Boy quickened his pace to keep up with him.

Their bags were heavy now, finally full after their many months on the road. Red Boy's bag pushed and bulged against his back, full of unearthly treasures dug from unexpected places, as well as a few interesting things he'd dug up just because he liked them. The other travelers had bags, too; or else massive chests that they carried with powerful arms; or perhaps trails of bubbles rolling behind them, each with something inside: a jeweled telephone, a book opening and closing like a butterfly's wings. Once there was a creature riding in a wagon, something that might have been a mouse if it had had the right features and the right number of paws. Though it might just have been a friend of the catlike creature who was tugging it along with her six spiderlike limbs.

No one spoke or turned to look at anyone else, but it was obvious everyone was going to the same place.

Then they passed through the trees, and he saw everything.

It was a valley of dreams, shaded by soft clouds that muted the moonlight. Beneath it, the blueish grass was dotted with campfires around which pavilions had been established.

Pavilion: that was another large word Red Boy knew. He knew it was a fancy tent, and these were the fanciest he'd ever seen. Some were made of silk, lace, or velvet. Others were covered in leaves stitched together with golden thread. Some were clear, made of something that hung and shivered like soap-bubble sheets in the wind. In the tents, shadowy figures moved through golden lamplight, and from their shapes and strangeness Red Boy knew that all these figures were Other Ones.

He and Big Beast didn't have a pavilion. They kept on walking down the long, gentle slopes of the valley, on and on through the moonlight past all the galaxies of tents, listening to the soft subvocal chuckles of friends meeting in the night and catching up on each other's travels. Red Boy wondered if Big Beast would stop (he seemed to have many friends), but he kept going down and down into the valley.

It was a long walk, but no one seemed to mind. The full moon rose slowly, and everyone walked down and down through its light towards the bottom of that vast bowl. And there, at the end of the long road, was an endless table.

It wound through the valley like a fat, lazy snake, glowing under silk lanterns that seemed to hang from nothing. Chains of flowers dangled in the air between them, casting flower-shadows on the table like a vision from fairyland.

The long table was made of thousands of smaller ones, Red Boy saw as they got nearer. Some were long, some short, some round, some square. Some were made of wood, others of metal, others of glass. Many were covered in cloths that looked like silk or velvet. They were set with different kinds of dishes, silver flashing in many styles and sizes, plates and napkins and fancy glasses like adults drank wine from. Some were simpler, with only a cup or a tin plate or a single wooden bowl. Some had chairs (folding ones, canvas ones, beautiful cushioned ones like the ones in museums). Others were surrounded by pillows piled high enough to sit on like chairs. Some tables had no seats at all, only the thick soft grass they stood on. Here some of the biggest of the Other Ones were easing themselves to the ground, heads towering over the tables without needing any seats at all. Their enormous starlit faces were peaceful as they looked up at the night sky, watching the golden dance of the thousands of curious fireflies coming to light and visit this strange dinner party.

Gradually, the Other Ones settled themselves, all chattering softly in their strange language wise as turtles and older than stones. There were all different dialects of that language (*dialect*, another word whispered from his fading past: a version of a language spoken only by some people).

He heard them only as parts of the rising babble, a great cacophony like thousands of birds over hundreds of tuning instruments.

Red Boy came shyly into the midst of these voices, following in Big Beast's enormous shadow, clinging to his friend's fur with one hand so he wouldn't get lost. Big Beast found them a table where one delicate chair stood beside a pile of cushions. He gestured for Red Boy to sit and plumped himself down on the cushions, arranging his massive limbs like a dragon settling around a mountain. He gave a sigh as he set his bag down, and Red Boy realized that his friend was as tired as he was.

He looked around. More of the Other Ones were filling in around them, coming in groups of two or three or five (and some alone) to take places of their choice. Slowly, Red Boy began to understand the different dialects of their bubbling, rumbling tongue, heard them all saying in different ways, **And here you are, friend... Here you are, friend; well met...** The lanternlight fell gently on fur and scales and feathers and skin in a thousand gorgeous shades. The yellow flash of fireflies flickered across their eerie eyes like distant lightning.

"Is it a party?" Red Boy whispered.

A feast, said Big Beast, patting his shoulder. (The impact, though gentle, was heavy enough to knock him sideways.) **The Feast of the Changes. It happens every year.**

Red Boy's stomach grumbled. A feast sounded good. He looked around but saw no sign of food, and there were no smells but the grass and the beasts and the cool night air. "Where's the food?" he whispered.

Big Beast's chortle rippled through the warm brown mountain of his fur. **We bring the food ourselves.** Opening his sack, he began to lay his treasures out on the table.

All around, the Other Ones were opening bags and boxes, taking out singing harps, silver kettles, blank-faced china dolls, robes made of fabric that moved without being touched. They oohed and aahed over each other's findings, trading things back and forth and holding them up to see them better by lamplight.

Red Boy didn't know what else to do, so he began to lay his things out, too. He kept back some of the regular treasures (a broken game controller, an action figure similar to one he'd had when he was little), but everything else he slowly put into the pile beside Big Beast's. There was a pencil made of cold, clear glass; a pirate's hat dotted with little mirrors (he'd found it in a dumpster); a stack of strange comic books with characters he'd never seen and absolutely no words. Big Beast unrolled the vast rug of purple plush they'd found in a trash pile, the silver plates that rang like chimes when they touched each other, the locket with a rose petal inside and a clasp shaped like a bird.

It took a long time for everyone to pile their treasures on the tables. When at last they'd finished, the Other Ones set to work with new energy, reaching out with strange and varied hands to take things from the piles and pull them apart.

Red Boy gasped at first, seeing the pale yellow Other One beside Big Beast bend all their silver plates in half. But Big Beast only laughed and took a shuffling pile of paper lace from the neighbor's pile in turn.

"What are they doing?" Red Boy whispered, hoping that the rustle and tingle of the Other Ones' work would cover the sound.

Making our feast, Big Beast said. Ripping the paper lace straight down the middle, he handed one piece to Red Boy. **Would you like one? It will be a good start.**

Hesitantly, Red Boy took the piece of lace. It was punched full of little holes, like the snowflakes his mother had taught him how to make once (she'd been sick in bed that day, working gingerly with nail scissors since they couldn't find the real ones). But the texture of it, now that he felt it, didn't feel like paper you could write on. It felt more like sugar.

Experimentally, he ripped off a corner and ate it. It tasted sweet, but very delicate, like moths' wings made of sugar. He nibbled a bit more, getting used to the taste. Then he rolled the paper lace into a large nest and began looking for things to put into it.

Everyone else was hard at work, creating and combining. Strange fruits were cut and tossed and arranged on silver platters, dusted with crumbled pages from gossamer books. Orbs of rubber sunlight were stretched and sliced, laid out on plates, sprinkled with the juice of things that weren't strawberries but smelled much better. Some of the Other Ones laid fires beside the tables. They roasted bits of their treasures on spits: strange vegetables dug from the gardens of museums, candied cotton, bread made of starlight, chestnuts from a silver tree that only appeared once a year. The smells were so rich that Red Boy's stomach growled more loudly. The Other Ones laughed and gave him things to eat. He shyly offered them his own treasures in return.

When the food was ready, the Other Ones stood up and sang a prayer in ringing chorus. Red Boy couldn't understand the words, but he felt the sentiment. He looked up at the sky, tears rolling, as he felt the moon begin to answer them. Then, all together, the Other Ones sat down and began to eat.

There was so much food that it seemed at first it would never be eaten. Some of the Other Ones were tiny. They nibbled like rabbits, picking and choosing from the littlest morsels. But others were huge, much larger than Big Beast. They ate with ravenous urgency, gobbling black pumpkins and bolts of silk fabric, gulping lilac wine from bowl-sized glasses. What they didn't eat they passed to their friends, who looked every hungrier.

Red Boy peeked sideways and saw Big Beast eating just as desperately, taking huge bites from his paper-lace pizza until it looked like a thin crescent moon. Remembering how sparingly his friend had always eaten, how careful he'd been to see Red Boy always fed, how scrupulously he'd saved whatever he could, Red Boy felt guilty for not realizing how hungry Big Beast must have been. His mother had often been hungry, too, in their life together, saving what she could for him and going without herself. He'd never known what to do about that, but he knew what he could do about this. So he ate as sparingly as he could, nibbling like the smallest of the Other Ones, occasionally nudging food toward Big Beast when his friend wasn't looking.

One of their neighbors, a lavender creature with tendrils on her head, peered over between bites of her marshmallow-gold sandwich and frowned. **You're not eating, Little Friend. Eat! It's the Feast of the Changes. You need to fill your stomach.**

This caught Big Beast's attention. He paused in his eating to scrutinize Red Boy's plate. **Eat, Red Boy.** His big brows lowered in concern. **There's plenty for all. Eat until you can't eat anymore. Then you'll see what happens next. It's why we came. Eat, eat!**

Eat! chorused the Other Ones.

Red Boy shyly obeyed, bringing his bird's nest towards him and raising it to take a bite.

Before, the taste had been delicate. Now he'd added

white chocolate drops melted from a fragrant candle, with drizzles of sweet brown syrup from a strange silver pitcher, and with slices of a succulent red fruit he'd found under a flowerpot in an abandoned greenhouse (weeks before, but still as juicy as the day he'd found it). The taste of it all was more decadent than a tall stack of pancakes on Sunday morning, more crumbling-sweet than the big pavlova he and Mother had once shared for a special treat. It tasted like everything he shouldn't have, everything that it was greedy to eat when others had so little. If he and Mother had had food like this, then they could have... they could have...

Red Boy, Big Beast murmured, **you are crying. Are you all right?**

Red Boy brushed tears from his face. "Fine."

His friend nodded uncertainly. **Eat, then. The best time is coming.**

So Red Boy put aside his guilt and began to stuff himself: shyly at first, and then more eagerly, tasting the year's treasures bite by bite and plate by plate. Every dish was totally different than the one before, and all of them somehow seemed perfectly cooked despite the lack of a kitchen. Each bite gave him a different sensation: a quiver in his stomach, a buzzing in his limbs, a sudden jolt and the urge to laugh. Soon he stopped worrying about anything. He only saw the food, the lamps, the night sky. He only heard silverware clinking and his neighbors murmuring happily, **It's good, it's good, it's good.**

He ate a pizza covered in shivering black seeds. He bit the fingers from a glove made of thin-flaked silver. He swallowed a star encased in jelly that burned hot down his throat and left a warm feeling in his stomach.

He ate and ate. Sometimes he set his fork down, but he

always picked it up again, feeling compelled to eat more. He couldn't stop. This had been the mission all along, he was beginning to realize. All the gathering and seeking, the long days of walking, the long nights asleep under strange swirling stars, all of that had been a buildup to this, the le-adup to one main event. Something important was about to happen, and Red Boy would be a part of it.

He ate until he finally began to see bits of his blue ceramic plate under the food. Till then, the Other Ones had been passing food to him so steadily that his plate had never had a chance to empty. All of them were slowing down, now. The pile of treasures, which had looked like it must last forever, was almost gone.

Seeing that, Red Boy suddenly began to feel full. He took a last bite of a gooseberry-cream tart and put his fork down. Leaning back, he laid his hands on his belly. When a neighbor offered him more food, he said grandly "No, thank you; no more."

The Other Ones seemed to agree. One by one, they leaned back, yawning and preening their grease-stained fur, wiping their hands and faces with napkins passed around by a creature like a very tall butterfly. Red Boy took a napkin, too, and sleepily wiped his face.

The Other Ones were whispering now, murmuring as they looked up at the moon, nudging each other. Something important was about to take place. They were about to see the purpose of the feast.

Big Beast finally set his fork down and accepted a napkin with a grateful nod. He wiped his face and fingertips delicately and set his napkin on the table. It's time, he murmured to Red Boy, smoothing his fur. Are you ready?

Ready for what? Red Boy wanted to ask. But Big Beast was standing up, and all the Other Ones were, too. He stood, too, and did what they did.

The first thing they did was look up at the bright full moon, which seemed to hang above their table as if waiting for them to do something interesting. When it had their attention, the moon pulsed bright silver. The Other Ones raised their hands and horns and tendrils and limbs and whirled, all spinning in unison as if they'd suddenly started hearing the same song. They bowed low to each other, joined hands and limbs and horns and tendrils, and began to dance.

Red Boy tried to follow the steps. He didn't really know how to dance. He'd heard music, of course, but no one had taught him what to do with it. But these steps were easy: one, two, three steps right; three steps left again; two steps back; two steps forward; bow, spin, repeat.

It went on and on like that. Some of the Other Ones were singing, humming, hooting a song he'd never heard before that somehow sounded familiar. Red Boy lost himself in the performance, feeling the world turn around him as he joined more and more into the rhythm of the dancing. Finally, breathing hard, all of them fell back into their seats. They laughed and held their stomachs and said to each other, **It was a good one this year, a good dance, a great feast!**

Then someone down the table called, in a buzzing voice bright with excitement and urgency, **Let us begin!**

Red Boy didn't know what to expect. The feast was swirling in his stomach, much less settled now, much less like food. For a moment, he wondered if he'd done wrong in sharing. Had it been wrong for him, a boy and not an Other One, to follow the long path with Big Beast and do all the things the Other Ones did?

But mostly he felt excited. Placing his hands carefully

on his whirling stomach, he watched eagerly as the purple Other One across the table suddenly stood up and cried, **Here it comes!**

With all the weaving tendrils on her head, it was difficult at first to see what was happening. Then the tendrils roiled and twisted, as if something were pushing out from behind them. There was a cool flutter of lilac wind, and then a dozen purple butterfly wings burst forth from all over the Other One's head.

Red Boy gasped. But his purple neighbor laughed and twirled and jumped into the air, her little wings fluttering rapidly to keep her afloat.

Beautiful! another neighbor cried. **How wonderful, such wings!**

As the changed one bounced and fluttered, other changes happened across the great gathering. One Other One grew a crown of bare branches with a ball of orange flame balanced in their midst. One (a snail-like being) grew rippling new stripes around the already-rippling edges of her body. A creature like a two-beaked crow now grew a third leg, and they laughed and chortled and murmured as if they'd been told a funny joke. As more and more Other Ones stood up, gaining rows of scales or tufts of feathers or sharp new horns or other wonderful things, Red Boy understood why this party was called the Feast of the Changes.

Soon even Big Beast stood up and shook his massive body, shifting his muscles till a ridge of golden spines emerged from the fur of his brown back. **Ah,** he said, sounding happy. **I've been waiting for these for a long time.** He saw Red Boy watching, and his look of happiness turned into puzzlement. **Red Boy, why aren't you changing?**

Startled, Red Boy saw that many of the Other Ones were watching him now, waiting for him to follow their example.

He opened his mouth to explain that he was human, that he couldn't change like they could. But then he considered.

He didn't really feel quite like himself anymore. He felt cramped and suppressed, as if not enough of him were out in the open. Suddenly he felt a very strong need to change that.

He tried to stretch, surreptitiously moving in his chair to get more space. Had his muscles fallen asleep? Though the dance should have woken him up. Anyway, it didn't feel like an outside muscle that was restless. It felt more like something inside his head.

The party grew quiet. Looking around, Red Boy saw that he was the only one who hadn't changed yet. Everyone was watching him expectantly.

He looked to Big Beast for a cue, but his friend only smiled, shaking his head, as if Red Boy should know what to do.

Red Boy looked around for inspiration. As he moved his head, he heard a loose jingling, as if several bells had been set free inside his mind. Then he felt a bright tingling low on his forehead, just above the bridge of his nose. He lifted his hand to touch the place.

Before he could, something blinked open on his forehead.

There! Big Beast said happily. **A beautiful start. A lovely first change, Red Boy.**

Beautiful, beautiful! the others cried. There seemed to be more of them now—or rather, Red Boy was seeing them too many times, from too many angles and directions. The world was bigger now, the stars brighter. The Other Ones looked fiercer and more magical, more otherworldly than any creature a human had a right to see.

At the same time, they didn't look strange at all. There

was something amazingly *familiar* about them: an ordinary, lovely feeling Red Boy had long known with Big Beast but never yet with any of the other Other Ones. He still felt wary (looking at their golden tusks, their three-foot talons, their lolling red tongues that wagged over the empty table). They were beasts, after all, and he was only human. But he thought, with time, that he might begin to know them. Perhaps that was the biggest gift of the evening.

Here, said the One with the wings on her head, handing Red Boy a large mirror. It's a good change. You came well prepared tonight.

Red Boy stared at the mirror in bewilderment and shock. Low on his brow, right where he'd felt the tingling, was a large ruby-red eye.

The Other Ones continued to chatter admiringly as Red Boy gently touched the lid of his new eye. It felt just like his other eyelids, with eyelashes just like the ones he had already. The eye was eye-shaped, quite normal besides its color, and blinked just like a normal eye would when his fingers got too close. But as he looked around, Red Boy understood that the new eye was what had added new depth to his vision, was adding shimmers and sparkles to the outlines of ordinary things—ideas of magic that hadn't been there before.

He looked himself carefully over, wondering if other changes were coming, but this seemed to be all for now.

You'll start slowly, said Big Beast, guessing his thoughts. **One change is enough for tonight. There will be time to collect and grow as you get older.**

Red Boy looked in the mirror again, blinking his new eye slowly, admiring its jewellike color. "Am I one of you now?" he asked hesitantly. "One of the Other Ones?"

Big Beast bowed assent, moonlight glancing off his new

golden spikes. But you already were, Red Boy. You were my companion all this year, living as I lived. How can you doubt that you were one of us?

Looking around, wondering if it could be true, Red Boy heard them clapping for him, smiling and nodding and murmuring approval. He felt the warm vibration of their applause against his bones, and for a long time he basked in the warm light of their acceptance. Then Big Beast took his hand, lifting him from his seat, and they all danced together, a great circle of joy under the stars.

Finally the sun in the distance began to rise, just barely under one or the other of the horizons, and the Other Ones began to yawn. Gradually they wandered off in different directions, some to their tents and some to other dances, some over the mountains and some along the valley and out of sight. There was no rhythm to their going, but all seemed to know exactly where they were headed, as if some purpose in their hearts were calling them.

"It's sad that they're all leaving," Red Boy said, as he and Big Beast waved goodbye to the last of their neighbors. They'd been a vast party, but the Earth was very big, and he knew it would be a long time before he saw them again.

It's necessary, Big Beast rumbled. **The world can't hold us all together most of the time. Some will walk in some places, others in others. But don't worry: we'll meet again next year, and we'll have the same feast, and we'll our friends and tell them our adventures.**

Red Boy nodded thoughtfully, understanding. "Which way will *we* go?" His mind flicked briefly to a woman with sad eyes, a woman who liked red and loved him. He wondered what she'd think of him, how he'd changed, the company he was keeping. But he still wanted to see her. It had been a long time. Perhaps she would like his new eye.

Big Beast cocked his head. **Why don't you choose the way? It's certainly your right after a year of following.**

Red Boy blinked his ruby eye. The world seemed to be changing around them, showing different directions, elements of the landscape he had not seen. But there were so many paths that he wondered which one to choose.

Then he realized there was a thrumming in his mind, a call softer than moonlight and older hills, telling him to go... *that way.*

I hear it, Red Boy said, his voice a startled echo. He pointed to a forest that had not been there moments ago, a wild wood growing at the edges of the valley. **We should go that way, I think.** Indeed, he saw a path of silver shining through the trees.

Big Beast bowed. **If you say so, then it is our path. Shall we go now? We can rest when we get tired.**

Red Boy thought of his mother, who might like to see her Other-One-son, and who at least would want to know what had happened to him. He wasn't sure he'd find her down this way, but his heart felt good, as if he finally were about to move in the right direction. **Let's go,** he agreed, taking the pack that Big Beast handed him. **I think we can go a long way before it's time to sleep.**

Big Beast rumbled, shaking his new spikes, and gestured courteously for Red Boy to precede him. Red Boy stepped onto the shining trail. It grew firm and solid beneath his foot, welcoming him fully into this world he'd only been a guest in. He took Big Beast's arm. As friends, they walked into the new year's journey.

Katherine Traylor is a US-born writer currently based in Prague, Czech Republic. Her writing is often fairy-tale-inspired with a strong focus on transformation. Her work can be found in the anthologies Slightly Sweetly, Slightly Creepy; Literally Dead: Tales of Holiday Hauntings; Dangerous Waters: Deadly Women of the Sea; Once Upon a Wicked Heart; *and* Gods & Services; *as well as* MYTHIC Magazine, Creepy Podcast, *and* Tales to Terrify. *She shares a home with her beautiful wife and three four-footed children. Follow her on Twitter (@amongthegoblins) or at her website, katherinetraylor.com.*

REMINISCENCES ON THE DEATH OF GEMAL THE SORCERER

R.K. Duncan

Sami was just putting the last touches on his painting of the Prophet Selim, who had seen God as a dove descending. The light streaming through the tall windows of the warehouse loft he shared with four housemates was brighter than the dawn of the canvas, but it made it easy to judge color, and Sami could move his canvas around the loft-circling balcony to get whatever light he needed as the sun moved. Now, in the mid-morning, the light came from the northeast, and he turned his easel to catch it sidelong, so that he cast no shadow over the work and didn't have to squint into the sun.

The painting was anachronistic enough to outrage any traditionalists once it was shown, set as it was in the modern Tula harbor, cranes at work in the background, dock workers, mostly Franks or Tatars, rushing to their shifts. Anyone likely to object to the inaccuracy would be more focused on the image of the prophet itself; Sami had painted him to closely resemble the banished sorcerer Gemal Atarwaz, with green turban, staff upraised to greet the descending dove, and a thick beard where the historical ascetic had shaved face and head to bare himself to god.

Below Sami, on the main floor, Touma was doing battle with the old, cantankerous wood-stove, wrenching the sticky flue handle open enough to let the fire build to cooking heat. Sweat dripped down the crimson fuzz on the buzzed side of their head, as they swore the damned thing must have rusted shut in last night's rain, and bent their tall, thin frame half inside the stove to look.

Both looked away from their work when Isaac burst in, arms full of bags and packages. His thin face was full of tearful emotion, and it made him look even younger than he always did. Isaac was the youngest of the five friends living here, a broad shouldered young man still awkward in his frame

He dragged scuffed shoes over the rough wood floor a moment before he spoke.

"Gemal is dead. I heard the readers cry it from the telegraph station. I brought everything we need for the memorial."

He tottered to the island of a threadbare eastern carpet in the center of the loft, and spilled his packages onto the round dining table as the others put away their work and came to join him. Touma brought plates, and in a few moments the table was laid with phyllo pastries, coils of cheese and apricot, parcels of honeyed pistachios. Mismatched glasses sat ready for the date wine and the mahia.

Touma glanced at the curtain rooms of their absent housemates. "Should we wait for everyone to get home? I know Ev' has an early shift today."

Sami answered before Isaac could voice the offense in his face.

"No. The dead come first. We begin the memorial as soon as we have heard of the death. That's the right way."

Isaac must have left whatever day-work he had found when he heard about Gemal. It was custom and prophet-given tradition for the close family of the dead to hold their remembrance at once on hearing of the loss, and while no employer would be giving time off to any mourner for the old sorcerer, all the housemates knew how Isaac felt about him.

Sami poured a drink of the harsh anise spirit and slammed it back in one gulp. Experience and his position as father figure for the little motley band let him control his throat and not cough at the shock. He took a coiled pastry and ate it in four precise bites, visibly attending to flavor and texture. He poured a glass of wine, lifting the bottle high so that the falling liquid caught the light with a sense of ritual and spectacle, then settled back into his chair. Both the younger ones had ceded him the high-backed armless one that he preferred. They left the mahia alone and took pastries and wine.

"Do you want to make the invocation, Isaac?" Asked Sami.

The young man nodded eagerly. Sami smiled benevolently at him and put a steadying hand over Isaac's on the table.

Isaac's voice shook a little with emotion. "Friends of Gemal the Sorcerer, what is the best—what is the worthiest story you can tell of him, that he may live in other hearts, since his is still and silent now?"

He swallowed and pulled out a smudged handkerchief to dab at not-quite-crying eyes.

Sami sipped his wine and stared into the middle distance, squinting at the bright windows. He tapped the fingers of his right hand on his plump belly as he thought.

"Gemal the Sorcerer refused to teach me once. This was when I was fifteen. I knew him to see of course. Everyone did, but we'd never spoken before. I'd just started to be told I was a bright kid, special, going somewhere. I started painting a little; a teacher gave me watercolors to play with after school, and my father took me to a few galleries on

Templeday sometimes, but I thought everyone telling me I was going to do something meant more than just art. Something bigger, and all I could think of was sorcery.

"I stopped Gemal in the square outside his tower one day and asked to be his apprentice. He said no; magic was a different way of seeing the world, and he couldn't teach it to me. But he told me to keep painting, that I might find a way of seeing that was just as good as his if I did. I would have been angry if my parents or teachers or anyone said anything so pat, but there was always that little charm in his voice that made me think he knew what he was talking about.

"He remembered me after, came to my shows at school. He bought two pieces once, for much more than they were worth, to help me pay for my last year. I'd seen all the masterpieces in his tower by then, so I knew it was for me, not because they were good enough to hang there."

He took another sip of wine and settled farther back into his chair.

Before anyone spoke, the door banged open again and this time Gerard, the longshoreman, was panting in the doorway. The light brown hair that marked him out as a Frank was wild, and his shirt was rumpled over his broad chest, his face redder than its perpetual sunburn. He looked a moment at he table.

"You've heard then."

"It's bad in the streets." He shook his head. "The purity priests and all their mob are throwing a rally in front of his old tower, and setting bonfires around it like they tried last year. And they're beating foreigners in the streets for a laugh, too."

He showed them his torn sleeve and the growing bruises under the tear.

"I got off easy. They're not out in this quarter yet, just down around the tower and the docks, and they didn't follow once I got away."

No one asked where the city Militia had been. They knew well enough how the black-caps felt about white-robe rallies and about foreign-born dockworkers.

Gerard slumped tiredly into a chair at the table and motioned the rest to go on.

"I can listen to stories as well as the rest of you, and I could use a bite anyway.

As if Gerard's report of bonfires had conjured it, a scent of acrid smoke began to creep in the open windows.

Isaac took his shot of Mahia fast and easy as water and leaned forward, elbows on the table, looking from face to face for his friends' approval as he talked.

"I worked for Gemal the Sorcerer, when he still lived in the city. I met him when I was living in one of the squats around his tower to keep off the street and he offered me work.

"I remember once I carried his bags shopping at the street market in Hilltop quarter, where all the country people brought their garden stuff and herbs and healing stones."

He shook. He had been shaking a little the whole time, as if his tears came in vibration instead of salt.

"He kept a thunderbolt for a pet, you know? Most of the time it just looked like a snake, so white it was almost blue. But when his, Gemal's temper was up, it would crackle instead of hissing, and it would shed light in a dim room. If you tried to touch it then, all your hair would stand on end. He let me play with it sometimes, when I was just a stupid street kid he hired to be kind."

He swallowed, looked down at the table as if it was a

picture of the memory. His hands played around opposite wrists, tracing invisible ropes or serpents.

"I only saw him let it loose once, there in that market. It was back twelve years ago, when the purity priests were making their first push against sorcery, caning people for witchcraft in the streets. We were walking in the market, him just looking like some old Rumish merchant in his robe and green turban, and then some fanatic in a white jacket pulled a knife and went for a poor old woman selling charms and sachets off a carpet. He was shouting about making the city pure. Everyone was shouting and pushing till I thought we'd be trampled.

"Gemal just pointed at the man, and he said something I'm sure I heard. It was something like 'vur-shim-shek,' but it sounds wrong when I say it."

His eyes flicked round the table again.

"There was big flash, so white and bright everyone was blind for a long while, and a crack so loud it was like being inside a bomb.

"When I could see again, the Pure was gone, just black ash, and the ground where he had been was dirty glass.

"It's funny you talking about how he told you what magic was, Sami. I asked him how he could do it, after he killed that man so easy, and he told me magic was like how recognizing someone all of a sudden makes you say their name, or like straightening a crooked painting. He could see how the world should change and the hard thing was to keep from doing it.

"The Pures never would have dared to go after you like that if he were still here, Ger.' Never."

Isaac took two of each pastry and ate them quickly in small, repetitive bites without a pause, hunching over his hands while he did.

The scent of smoke grew worse, and a slight haze crept over the sun as the friends sat and digested another memory.

Gerard took a deep drink of date wine, swallowed a sweet pastry in one long bite, and washed it down with mahia.

"I never knew the old man the way you all did, but I remember his fireworks. He used to set off fireflowers all green and silver and red over his tower on Templeday. And I remember how the top of his tower was always lit up like a green moon.

"I used it to steer my way home my first year in the city, when our apartment was in the wharf quarter and I had a job sweeping at Mansi's bakery after school. It was the only way I could pick through all those little alleys without signs in the dark. My parents made me learn the script before we came so I could read the signs, you know. So I could try and fit in, but it didn't do much good. They couldn't teach me how to talk, or how to find my way at night.

"Gemal the Sorcerer's tower was my first friend in Tula, before any of the other children talked to me."

Sami and Touma glanced out the windows. The smoke was thick over the city now, hazing the noon sun as it blew south from the harbor.

"Shut the windows with me, would you, Isaac?" asked Sami.

They both stood and circled the big room, winding the tall casements closed. It would get hot, and Sami drew several curtains to keep some sun out, but heat was more bearable than the smoke; whatever was burning out in the city smelled dirty.

When they came back to the island of the table and carpet, there was a long moment of awkward looking out and guessing, and the talk drifted to inconsequential things for a while, everyone taking the excuse not to think of what was going on outside. It was rude of larger problems to intrude on the intimacy of a private remembrance.

Touma was still coughing after throwing a big shot of mahia back too fast when Ev' stumbled in, sweat on her face, ash on her nurse's red and drab uniform, blood still under her nails. Her mouth was tight and her eyes were wide and red-rimmed.

If Sami played the father for the loft's patchwork family, Ev's was closest to a mother for the rest, and seeing her so obviously shaken worried them all.

Sami and Isaac were up at once and helped Ev' to the table. Sami ceded her the softest chair, and Gerard brought a glass of water, still cold from the stone cistern.

"What happened, Ev'?" asked Isaac, leaning close.

She took a long drink before she snapped.

"They fucking burned Gemal's tower. The whole block he built around it, the hostels and the squats farther out that people never got chased out of. It's all burning, and the tower. And the Pures won't let anyone try to put it out."

She paused, and stared at nothing, and trembled for a little while. Everyone was shaken. Ev' was usually iron control in a small frame, only letting loose on the dance floor. Only Sami had ever seen her cry.

Ev' went on, voice shaking while her white-knuckled hands were steady, doubled around her water glass. "They're...They're killing people who get out of the squats. Just beating them in the streets. Some of them, the white-robe thugs, came to the hospital to stop us treating 'sinners' and 'witches.'

"I had to get out."

She stared ahead at nothing. She fingered the row of

steel rings that marched along the curve of her right ear, slid down to where a tattoo peeked above the line of her uniform on her neck. They all knew why she couldn't have stayed longer with Pures hunting in the hospital.

"They think they own the city now, and the militia are letting them do what they like. Even when the doctor called, they still wouldn't throw the Pures out."

"Isn't anyone fighting back?" demanded Touma. "The wharfs aren't white-robe territory. Is the whole city just rolling over?" They slapped a fist into their open palm.

Ev' shrugged, defeated. "Sure, some idiots are out there getting beaten. We had plenty of them in the hospital, next to the burned ones."

"We've got to do something," said Touma. They stood so fast their chair fell back and clattered on the threadbare rug. "If those fuckers think they own the city, we'll show them they don't. Now, before it gets worse. Who's fucking coming with me?!"

They pulled on heavy black boots. Clubwear, but intimidating.

Isaac rose, looking pale. "You're right. Let's show them whose city it is." His voice was more tentative than the words, and he glanced back at the table, but he didn't sit down.

"You just going to let them scare you off the streets, Ger'?" prodded Touma.

Gerard hesitated, looking from the exhausted Ev' to Touma by the door.

"I'll take care of Ev'," said Sami. "You go."

Gerard sighed and rose. He went to his curtained bedroom and returned with a long prybar over his shoulder. He had never taken off his work boots.

The three went out, keeping close and chattering nothings to pep themselves up.

Sami stood behind Ev' in the quiet loft, rubbing her shoulders. After a little while of it, he brought a cool cloth from the sink for her hands and face and sat beside her at the table.

Ev' poured a shot and took it. There was still soot on the glass when she set it down.

"Hell, I'll tell a story. Why not?"

Sami nodded, and pushed the pastries toward her.

"I remember the first time I saw Gemal the Sorcerer, in the line for costume night at The Lillies. I hadn't gotten tired of cutting up my uniforms for the club yet then, so I was a nurse. When he got into line a bit behind me, I thought Gemal was just someone in costume as him, green turban, fake beard, robe covered in stars, but he was close enough that when I kept looking, I could see the stars move in the cloth.

"I think most people didn't realize it was him until the doorman said he was too old and tried to keep him out. I had just gone in, and I turned around when Gemal laughed. He grew up tall, twelve feet maybe, and he was all covered in black shadows, a lord of the underworld with three burning lampads, beautiful and naked and burning on leashes in his train."

She tapped her foot with nerves or remembered rhythm, or both.

"He kept changing shapes the whole night. Sometimes he was djinn, all fire and smoke, or a dog-headed man, or a serpent twisting through all the dancers. He would offer to be dog for anyone who had a leash, or turn ears and tails and horns real for the evening.

"I always liked dancing with him, because he never got tired and he never expected anything. Lots of men, especially on costume nights, just came to look pretty. They'd dance a bit to show off and get sweaty, and then lean at the bar and make come-ons, but Gemal never stopped. He was always still going when they kicked us out for curfew, and if someone needed seeing home, he'd take them in his carriage that went without horses or just walk beside to keep the watch off.

"He came with me and few other friends from nurses' school one night to a place that opened at dawn and gave you free drinks with breakfast to get around the temperance bell, and we got stopped by Militia looking for a payoff. I was afraid it would be a vice charge, until Gemal stepped up looking like a colonel and sent them scampering. He was always good for a laugh and making big men fall down to earth."

Her story trailed off, and by the drifting of her eyes, Sami could guess she was back at the hospital again. A bad shift had a long hangover.

⸎

The streets were full of smoke as Gerard, Isaac and Touma headed north toward the wharf-quarter, where Gerard had been for his dawn shift, where the tower was burning. A light breeze off the water blew the smoke over the converted warehouses and factories of their home quarter, and the tops of newer tenements were lost in it.

They were far from the only ones in the street. Uncertain people, young, most of them visibly pierced or tattooed, gender-bent, or otherwise alternative, milled around outside their lofts and smoke-filled apartment blocks. There were a few paler, light-haired Franks like Gerard, but most of them had been gentrified out farther west as the neighborhood was converted for the hungry young offshoots of

Tula's middle class.

The first time they passed a knot of people, Touma shouted. "What are you all standing around for? The fire's at the sorcerer's old tower. Fight's there too, come on!"

Most people did not follow, and the streets emptied as they came closer to the tower and the square before it. A roaring sound drowned idle conversation, and the heat became a weight, squeezing sweat out of them like sponges until the soot clung to them like a second skin.

When they came out of the narrow streets onto the square, they saw the tower burning. The whole height of the spire was wrapped in fire, and flames poured out of every window, though the stone was not consumed. At the tower's feet, only black ashes and a few half-burned beams were left of the wooden houses Gemal the Sorcerer had built once and let free to any who needed them. In the middle of the square, as close to the burning tower as the heat allowed, a solid bloc of white-clad people packed around a makeshift platform, and one robed figure exhorted them from it; a tall man, shaved smooth on head and face, shaking his scarred hands in the air as he screamed over the roar of the flames and the rushing wind that pulled everything toward the burning tower.

The counter-protest was patchy, little knots of people who drifted closer and farther as the edges of the purity mob shifted. Locals, half-homed or homeless in the fire kept their knots separate from dockers coming off shift, and the young people waited farther back as they drifted from other quarters, looking and wondering and not sure who they were more afraid of. At the west edge of the square, a line of black-capped militia waited, hands on batons or pistols, but they made no move to stop the brewing fight.

"Look," said Isaac. "It's that mad bastard Tadros. When

did he come back out in public?"

"If we're still telling stories," Touma said, "I remember when Gemal had that 'debate' with Tadros right here, where they've put up the stage. Gemal challenged him to prove that everything they say about sorcery and foreigners and country people and women and everyone they hate really was out of the scriptures."

The other two leaned close to hear him over the shouting of the priest and the noise of the wind.

"I watched it, and Tadros had the best of it to begin with. You know how the Pures always talk about 'in the tradition of the prophets,' and 'our forefathers believed,' and all that mealy mouthed cover for 'Tula for the Tulasa and fuck the country people'. Gemal knew all the prophets back and forth, though I don't think he ever went to temple, and he quoted at Tadros and challenged all his nonsense, but Tadros just talked over Gemal until he had the whole crowd with him, ready to beat some poor devils out of the city, so Gemal made him scream like a bird every time he tried to lie. He shouted till he was red in the face, but it only came out like a hawk screeching, and Gemal would just ask him to repeat, with the chapter and verse number, please.

"Everyone laughed and cheered for Gemal, and they saw through all the Pures' lies for a day, at least."

"Maybe," said Gerard, "but it was after that debate the Pures really started hounding Gemal, and pressing to have him exiled. They got their way, no matter how stupid Gemal made them look."

"I wish we could shut them up like he did, though," said Isaac.

They had been drifting closer to the Pures, along with a thin crowd of other onlookers, and now the mob turned and noticed them. It only took moments for chanting to break out.

"Tula for the Tulasa!

"Job stealers out!

"Beggars off the street!

"Witches out!"

Rocks and bottles flew, mostly at visible foreigners like Gerard. The purity mob put out spearing tendrils, driving into the crowd, and people they came close to gave ground and ran.

A bottle hit Gerard, not hard enough to shatter before it hit the ground. "No way to do this," he muttered.

He shook himself and shouted, pushing air with his big chest. "Dockers front! Make a fucking line!"

He ran for the front, prybar up over his head like a standard, and a few began following him. He shouted at other dockers from his own shift or the later one, and they came at his call. Touma and Isaac came close behind.

"Come on." Gerard began to sing. "Up, up, and up, we lift 'em."

Other dockers joined the forming line and the song. "Down, down, and down we drop 'em."

As the line of dock-workers solidified, the rest of the crowd pressed in behind them, and they pushed the Pures back toward Tadros' platform to the rhythm of the working tune.

⚊⚊⚊⚊⚊⚊⚊◆◆⚊⚊⚊⚊⚊⚊⚊

While Ev' showered off the grime of her hospital shift, Sami returned to his canvas. The hazy light of smoked-over noon fit the dawn light he had painted. The canvas almost shone in its own twilight. It looked different now than when he had left it. Cloudy somehow, like something waiting to be born instead of almost finished. He passed a cloth lightly over the dry part in case soot had settled there, but it still seemed to have gained the quality of a thunderhead about to break, and he could not see how to restore it.

He returned to the saint's face for a few strokes, thickening the white beard and adding whimsy to the smile, making the image more perfectly Gemal than he had planned. It felt right in his bones, like a something pushing back into place.

He added detail to the workers in the background. He had intended them shadowy, but now a few lighter strokes brought out fair hair or long Tatar moustaches, worn; torn clothes and tired postures made them solid, and helped push back the feeling of ominous potential that had overtaken his canvas.

<hr>

With lines solidified, the Pures and the protesters shouted back and forth. Tadros' voice boomed from his bullhorn. The heat still sheeting off the burning tower felt like a wall that hekd the protesters back and shielded the fanatics.

"Now is the time to clean the city, faithful of the Prophets!" Tadros shouted, and the Pures stopped shouting slogans to hear him.

Touma shook their head and spat. A tap on a tall shoulder and a shouted request got them lifted between two solid dockers, high enough to shout over the crowd, and for their half-shaved, half turquoise head to be seen.

"See, faithful and pure," screamed Tadros, " the foreigners and deviants who will ravage your wives and daughters? Who will ruin your city and leave you homeless? Penniless?"

Touma drew in breath and shouted back before the crowd could drown them out. "Damn right this deviant will give your wife a better time than you can! Do you mean the first one Tadros, who took you to court for beating her? Or the new one you made cut out her tongue because women ought not speak in the temple?"

The Pures shouted murder after that, but Touma knew they'd scored a point. The purity priests spoke about desert fathers castrating themselves to keep virtuous, and silencing women as the same, but even among the rank and file streetfighters, it was viewed uneasily. Most of them wouldn't dare tell their wives to do it, or marry the kind of fanatic who really would, so they made up for their failure of virtue with violence, and threw themselves against the docker's line with new fury.

Touma kept shouting taunts and encouragement, but they weren't sure who could hear above the din.

———————•◦•———————

Only one last thing, and the painting would be finished. Sami mixed blue and his purest white and twisted a thin line around the figure's wrist, a serpent, or a thunderbolt. His brush dragged for a moment, as if there was a roughness in the canvas or a weakness in his arm, and then it ran on and finished the line. He stepped back. It was done. God the dove descended to Tula's harbor, just as it would be at dawn, the cranes already busy, the streets empty but for the saint and workers rushing early to their shifts.

It looked alive, and different. Now that he looked again, he knew the light over the bay was never so diffuse, the clouds never so pearly, that a little break of sun could not pick out one figure so and leave all the rest shaded. But everything he had done was right next to the rest. A different world, or a different way of seeing this one. He had undone the thunderhead unfinished-ness of before, and now the truth shone on the canvas.

At last the protest turned to a battle. The militia moved in behind the protesters, and the Pures took the signal and pressed in. With sticks, bottles, knives, and burning brands from the still blazing tower, they came on, and they rolled through the dockers into the crowd. Gerard laid down one and two and three with his bar, but the press of the crowd behind him pushed too many inside his reach and the went down under the weight of them.

They would be on Isaac in moment. He pulled his knife and snapped it open, but he was no fighter, not even when he had been on the streets. He tried to be ready.

Something tingled on his wrist, and the word that had never come right before fell back into his mind, like the name of an old friend.

The world was crooked, but he could push it right again.

A big white-jacketed man with a thick stave was right in front of him, stick raised to attack.

"Shimshek Vurmak!"

There was a flash. A crack so loud it was like being inside a bomb.

When Isaac could see again, white-clad figures were scattered like torn pages, and more were sitting up dazed, or running. Militia behind were shouting something for people to disperse, but there was clear ground right in front of him.

He found Gerard, groaning among other fallen dockers, and went to him. Gerard was bruised and battered, but he was breathing and his eyes open at Issac's touch. He reached up to Isaac's left hand.

"Look at you."

Isaac could feel a tingling again where Gerard grabbed

his wrist, and he looked down and there was Gemal's lightning bolt, still twined around his wrist, not gone, not a dream or a fluke. He could feel it, how to make it strike again.

He followed Gerard's eyes to the tower.

It was not burning anymore, and there was no mark of fire on it.

"Can you make the top light, do you think?" asked Gerard. "Or set off fireworks?"

Isaac felt himself smile, and he felt the world balanced, waiting for his touch.

"Let's find out."

The tower door opened for him, and he helped Gerard up. They walked across the emptying square together.

R. K. Duncan is a fat queer polyamorous wizard and author of fantasy, horror, and occasional sci-fi. He writes from a few rooms of a venerable West Philadelphia row home, where he dreams of travel and the demise of capitalism. His other full-time job is keeping house for himself and his live-in partner. Before settling on writing, he studied linguistics and philosophy at Haverford college. He attended Viable Paradise 23 in 2019. His occasional musings and links to other work can be found at rkduncan-author.com.

DILATION

Jay Caselberg

Lifetimes and memories
Pass here
Between the stars
As I view your distant images
Now beyond me
Now behind me
And crumbled long to dust

Jay Caselberg is an Australian author and poet whose work has appeared around the world and been translated into several languages. From time to time, it gets shortlisted for awards. He currently resides in Germany and can be found at www.caselberg.net.

The Backyard

Kayla Whittle

Something crashed in the backyard and Penelope's television shuddered and died. She learned then that in emergency situations, instead of fight or flight, she chose to freeze, rooted to her sofa as she waited for a follow-up explosion or the far-off wail of sirens. Instead, a fierce crackle tickled her ears as green light washed over her living room walls.

The space brightened around her, like a rogue, sickly sun had broken through the night. In Penelope's blank corpse of a television screen, her reflection stared back at her. She lived alone; there was no one to consult about what to do next. Half-suffocated by nerves, Penelope stood, wiping her hands on her plaid pajama pants. Her heart fell back somewhere onto her couch, leaving behind enough blank numbness to keep her from panicking.

Accompanied only by the screen door's rusted shrieks, Penelope eased into the backyard. A few dozen steps from the porch, someone lay sprawled on her lawn. Farther beyond that sat a spaceship. That was the best word for it, though Penelope's eyes burned if she looked at it directly. The green light, stronger out here, hummed through her teeth. She tried to focus on the figure, but it hurt to perceive them, too—until they made a noise that sounded painful in any language. Penelope blinked, and it felt like her vision cleared, or some link had been severed that'd connected her eyesight to her brain. The sound burrowed into the folds of her occipital lobe, and through it, somehow, she knew the figure was alone, too.

They were pale and small and shone like starlight. They had two hands, two legs, and a mouth that was shut tight in an anxious frown. Every tense line of their body spoke of hurt, enough to make Penelope's heart settle right back into her chest so she could start thinking of how to help. The dark was quiet around them as she moved closer; her pants dampened with early morning dew when she knelt.

"I'm not here to hurt you," Penelope said, reaching forward. Her fingers twitched back a time or two when the stranger shifted. The movement might have been breathing, but it looked more like they were turning their head, tasting the air.

Their hands darted toward hers; a flicker of fear fought through the calm the noise had instilled in her. Their grip was soft like lamb's wool, and their frown smoothed into something serene. Their lips parted and another sound emerged, a rumble like drumbeats and the whistle of a broken flute. Their jaw tensed, muscle rippling as if sorting out the solution to a new problem. When their lips moved again, they spoke.

"Your music is beautiful," they told Penelope, and then they fell asleep.

⚫◦⚫

Penelope considered phoning the police, or the National Guard, or maybe her sister, who could at the very least stop by to confirm she could also see the alien. But the phone had died the same sudden death as her T.V., and her home sat alone, a few miles outside of town. No one had arrived to investigate the disturbance; she was on her own. As she had most other times when she'd come to that conclusion over the past few years, Penelope sighed and pretended she wasn't bothered by it at all.

She rubbed her sternum, that hesitant place that'd calmed due to her unexpectant visitor. Although her head remained clear, Penelope was still capable of worrying about the possibility of hallucinations, and the inevitability of extraterrestrial life, and the stillness of the figure on her lawn. She didn't know what they'd meant about the music, but that didn't matter much, because she realized she couldn't stand the thought of leaving someone without help when they were alone, too.

It was easy to take them inside. She'd been worried about straining her back, but their body was light as the air they'd come hurtling through. Penelope put the stranger up on her sofa, tucking a blanket around them. Poured them a glass of water, mostly to make herself feel useful. She didn't know how best to host an alien. Night ticked into dawn, and she considered going to see if her car would start, when the visitor stirred.

"It's so quiet here," they said. Their frown had returned.

When they held out their hands, Penelope took them. She'd come too far to hesitate over that contact now. Something about the connection relaxed the alien, which she hoped would either keep both of them calm, or soothe Penelope into waking from this dream.

———————————◆◆◆———————————

Penelope startled upright with a crick in her neck, the rest of her body protesting that she'd slept half-hunched over the couch. The stranger watched her, their pinched expression looking as sore as she felt.

"I'm sorry for any damage caused by my ship," they said.

"It's my fault. It went so quiet up there. I don't think there are many of you around here."

Penelope was silent for a moment, thinking about how this was not in fact a dream, and she didn't care about the state of her property at all, and the alien still held her hands. They squeezed, gently, and Penelope heard chimes.

"Why are you here?" Penelope asked.

"My love is gone," they said, the music between them souring, discordant. "I've traveled far, searching for a way back to her. Somewhere, I will find the doorway that leads to her. Not on this planet, I think. Everything is too muted here."

Penelope knew little of loss but much of loneliness. This stranger had crossed galaxies, solo, in pursuit of something beautiful. Sympathy eased her worry, but something uglier lurked beneath that felt like the acid sting of jealousy.

Penelope went to pour them another glass of water, though they hadn't touched the first one.

⬤◆⬤

After brief consideration, mostly concerning the lack of space in her home, Penelope decided to let the alien stay. Once they could stand and move again, they helped tidy the house, wandering about with her blanket tucked around their shoulders. She liked giving extended company a chance, as unexpected as they'd been, and the two fell into a routine as easily as the alien had fallen from the sky.

The stranger never attempted any ship repairs until at least half an hour after Penelope had her first cup of coffee. Penelope fired up her computer and worked remotely all day, as usual, while dully methodic thuds echoed from outside. There were no neighbors to be bothered by the noise. Every few hours, around the time Penelope should have given herself a break but was more often than not trapped within her inbox, a rolling crescendo would peep through her screen door. She would stand, crack her neck, and go out to greet her alien. They would hold onto each other for the briefest moments, only long enough to stave off some of the stillness the visitor hated so much.

At night, they sat together in front of the new television Penelope had hauled in from town after she'd jumpstarted her car with her generator. The alien never ate, but they held her hand gently and slumped down into the music that emerged wherever their skin connected. It was beautifully incomprehensible, just like the stories they told her. Places like Earth that ran so quiet they sent the alien into something close to shock—though, they admitted, this was the first time they hadn't been able to gather themselves together in time to prevent an unplanned, violent landing. There were planets filled with so much sound no one could hear anyone else. Galaxies overpopulated and others emptied. Doorways found and stepped through, with no one waiting for her visitor on the other side. Not yet.

Penelope told them about her life, too. The good parts, the family members living on the other side of the state and the friends who'd message her during the week. Her perpetually busy sister, unable to schedule much but ready to drop everything for an emergency. She showed them how sunsets looked from her back porch and described, in meticulous detail, the excellent deal she'd gotten on her cable package.

She worried her stories held no weight in comparison to her visitors'. An unfounded worry, maybe, because they always listened with the highest reverence, eyes closed as if her words held a hidden melody perceivable only by the alien.

One evening, Penelope reached for their hand first. After a day of straining her eyes against blue light, she wanted to hear the chiming clash of notes only her stranger could emit. They held onto her, tighter than before.

"Penelope," they said. "I wouldn't mind having a friend by my side while I search. Perhaps there is a doorway out there for you, too."

Penelope had never boarded an airplane before. She thought of the shining, impossible ship sitting in her yard and the kind, impossible friend sitting in her living room. The alien crossed galaxies for love; Penelope wondered what it would be, the thing waiting on the other side of a doorway that might fix everything for her. If she didn't know before she searched, she wasn't sure she'd recognize the right doorway even if she found it.

"I couldn't," Penelope admitted. "The offer, though. I appreciate it."

They tilted toward one another, and the music swelled as the television switched to a commercial break.

"It's complete," they said. "As complete as it will be, here."

Parts of the spaceship had dulled, scarred by the harsh landing. The stranger remained certain it would hold together well enough to fly to another planet, another doorway, at least. One more step in their interminable path.

This time, when their hands met, the notes between them sounded jumbled. Complicated, like Penelope's emotions. Her happiness seeped through, knowing her friend could be seen off safely. Her nerves lingered as she inched back toward what life had been for her before a spaceship tore through her yard.

"Good luck," Penelope said. "If you need me again, I'll

be here."

"Thank you for your help," her friend said. "But I will not return."

They chimed, and rang, and finally, pulled away. Penelope stood behind her screen door, watching until the crackle of the ship's engines faded.

When she retreated to the living room, Penelope discovered her television had died again.

Afterward, in the quiet, Penelope tried making it less obvious something had crashed on her property. She planted a garden where the ship had once rested. She dug a hole to bury a few damaged parts left behind. She purchased a new television, left it inside the box, and then hammered a sign into her front yard.

A month later, Penelope had a bag packed and the rest of her things in a storage facility. Her sister had a copy of the key. She'd keep an eye on Penelope's things, she'd promised. For as long as was needed.

Loneliness left a lot of time for thinking. Penelope had decided she wanted to become the sort of person who knew exactly what doorway they needed to search for.

Penelope left, chimes ringing in her ears.

Kayla Whittle has previously had short stories published in Uncharted Magazine *and* The Colored Lens. *She also has stories in the anthologies* Beyond the Veil *(Ghost Orchid Press), and* Of Fate & Fury *(Silver Wheel Press), as well as* Dangerous Waters, Daughter of Sarpedon, *and* Seers and Sibyls, *all out with Brigids Gate Press. Her work has been featured on Flash Fiction Podcast. Most often she can be found on Instagram @caughtbetweenthepages or on Twitter @kaylawhitwrites.*

DANCE, DIPLOMACY, AND DISSOLVED FAITH

Anna Clark

The night was stale, and no one had asked the queen to dance. I was no practiced courtier, but they were doing it wrong.

She sat atop the dais, surveying the wasteland of dance floor down a curved nose, dark eyes rebuffing the witch lights' gleam, long fingers stroking a castle cat, regal and inscrutable as she. Beneath her study, what dancers persisted swayed like seaweed anchored to storm-worn rocks, frayed and diffuse. Those with a better read on the currents shoaled along the walls. They didn't dance, but neither were they still; the moon chamber was stalked by agitation, tilted heads and sideways glances, well-shod feet tapping to flee.

Priestess of a vanquished adversary that I was, I should have been shrinking in a corner, but fascination rose buoyant above all other emotions. I'd dwelt so long in the rarefied world of deities, and the queen was substance and presence; even cushioned in magic and the envelope of subject demands, she was accessible in a way rarely encountered by the devout.

Alon touched my sleeve. "We should leave. We'll make no deals tonight."

A witch light hung like stardust by his ear, gilding the folds of his silk gown with pearl and tracing silver thread into the new crease lines on his face. His mouth was drawn. Alon was a practiced courtier, but navigating these waters had eroded him.

"You go," I said. "I'll see the night through. I can't return home to greet our supplicants with empty hands for another prayerless harvest." Guilt supplanted intrigue. How much of my offer stemmed from confidence I could sway the court into restoring the severed link to our deity, and how much from preoccupation with the woman who'd broken it? My eyes strayed to the queen again. I wondered if she liked to dance.

"It's late," began Alon, before noticing the tilt of my head. His jaw clicked. "Don't look at her so long. She's an uncanny way of noticing, even in a crowd."

And didn't that make it hard to look away? Sometimes, I thought her stare lingered as mine dropped. The thought was fanciful and traitorous, born from a hunger to know interest returned—if only in measured curiosity. The goddess's gaze, in its encompassing knowledge, never sought answers.

"I mean it, Seri," said Alon. "Stop. We want her advisors' attention, not hers."

I wasn't so sure. Most here had done well by the dissolution of the Atuevez Order, this island's sect of the goddess, and those that lost out saw the fate of the Faith-Allied Fleet and kept their distance. "Because that's going so well."

He huffed. Witch lights didn't flatter the exhausted.

"Go," I told him.

Surrender dropped his chin, bowed deeper the curve of his shoulders. Two moons ago, when the solstice sun spurned the horizon and our ship was fresh in the harbor, Alon would have baulked at ceding the night. Now, all he offered was, "Be careful. Better to flee home and pray in empty temples than be dead and beyond prayer entirely. The goddess wouldn't ask more."

When he was gone, I was still turning over his truth; she wouldn't, however much I wished it of her.

People of influence congregated towards the back of the chamber, away from their sorcerous ruler. As was the style here, their gowns were jeweled with purloined temple ornaments, repurposed but undisguised. They flaunted their power in goddess-eye brooches, but the expanse of oiled floor between them and the dais spoke its limits.

An entreaty: *return our goddess, and with her loose, live in dread of two great women.* Little wonder they turned us away. Alon was right to predict no deals from this faction.

Time for a different tack. He knew officials, but I knew gods, and with the power to splinter a hundred masts and lock a deity apart from her devoted, the queen was close—but crucially different—to the latter.

She gave me nothing as I bent obeisance before her step, no crack in her countenance, no hitch in the rhythm of her stroking. The cat yawned at me.

"Your Majesty, I am Seri of the Kafalai Order. I sailed from Fenarin to speak with you on a matter of much importance to my people."

The cat jumped from the queen's lap and stalked away. Not quite a wrathful omen, but hardly auspicious. She tracked its progress into the arms of an attendant, tapping a finger on the green satin arm of her chair, before pressing me beneath shadowed eyes. "So speak."

"Thank you, Majesty." Here was my gap in the clouds to present our case. The goddess had required more chanting. From my years of service at the Kafalai temple, I was good at distilling miracles from higher beings, but my insides shriveled to play another supplicant, offering prayer, begging deliverance for my deity behind clasped hands and hardened knees. I needed her to see me, to know me as a person besides my vassal state. A question caught me: how long had I wanted to be something other than a priestess? I didn't know.

"In truth, I have two requests," I said. "One for my people, and one for myself. For my own—will you dance with me?"

Quiet. Hers, but also rippling out to encompass all in our circle of hearing, shifting tides convening through breathless, vicarious terror. They couldn't ignore me now. A vision of Alon shook his head, the icon of rebuke.

She was a winter lake, smooth surface hiding fathoms, and I sensed the deep peering out. I might have been in terrible error, but the flare of nerves felt exquisite. One side of her mouth lifted into a sickle moon smile.

"I will," said the queen.

She stood; music stuttered. Her voice, unraised: "Continue." Timidly, it did. Her walk was fluid, controlled, and I was left in the transfer of her stillness, anticipating.

Then she was before me, and I could see the play of muscles beneath draped summer fabric, the elegant slope of her shoulders framed over a wide neckline, winged collar bones, the dip between breasts. Notable in their absence on her person were repurposed symbols of the goddess. Traces of the dissolution gilded everyone but its architect, leaving her stark, embossed in rumors and reputation beyond ordinary luster. I should have seen a jailor, her magic a stockade blocking the divine from the pious. But here, close enough to read her blood's tempo under the lines of her throat, it was hard to see the queen as anything less—or more—than a person. Who was I to judge one who'd marshalled a collapsing state and halted a holy war?

"You look beautiful tonight, Majesty," I said.

"And not the other nights you watched me?"

"Then, too."

The other side of her mouth curled up—a full smile. Still dangerous. We were similar in height, level eyes and level lips as she drew close, placed a palm on my waist, thumb brushing ribs. A touch like magic. I rested my arm above hers, hand to her shoulder, and hoped for magic adjacence.

The answer to my question was clear in her first assured steps: yes, she liked to dance. And it was well we were proficient, with melody and rhythm striking such weak guides. Notes flowed tepid around us, lacking the convection of early evening and bypassing the warm languor appropriate for this hour on tension-stiff fingers. No matter. If this wasn't the transcendent musicality favored by gods, I was grateful. We didn't fly or float, ethereal beings, but danced to the beat of the ground, close and tangible.

I wanted to be closer. My oaths were to another.

The queen's hand slid higher on my back. "Tell me your second request."

Even on solid, temporal dance floor, there was no escaping my divine purpose. I'd have sworn the goddess had a hand in its raising were she not locked beyond reach, leaving only the queen's machinations at play.

The words I had prepared were plain. Too many supplicants to the temple of Kafalai, whose twisting spires I called home, couched their prayers in the language of abasement, repetitions of 'most humbly' and 'your unworthy servant' stirring a soup so thick that the sediment obscured intention.

"Fenarin misses our goddess. I'm here to ask for her release."

She instigated a sharp turn, skirt flaring, drawing me with her. "You're asking me to unbind the wind behind the sails of a fleet that stormed my shores."

No surprise steeped her tone, but a summer storm brewed thickly around us. The last clinging weeds of other dancers washed into the crowd.

"The goddess was no orchestrator," I said, acceding to her lead up the chamber, away from the dais. "Any gusts of hers manifested from sailors' prayers and were granted without malice towards you. She sees the worshipper. Nothing else." *Never* anything else. For Alon, born to mercurial parents who weighed their children's contributions and returned affection in correspondence, that parity was her most cherished aspect. It spoke badly of me that it wasn't mine.

"They sailed here to restore the goddess's shrines," said the queen.

"As pretext for conquest and enrichment."

She laughed, dispelling none of the threat—but what a lovely timbre. "You put your case so eloquently. Give a greedy people back their weapon of a god."

"She's goddess to more than the invaders. My land had no part in the alliance, and the goddess means many things to different people: hope and harvest, an arbiter who won't act for coin, a healer who won't cure an ailment at the price of starvation. Your people have you to magic the land. We rely on gods for our miracles."

Another pivot, quick and smooth as a hawk dropped into its dive. Was I a caught rabbit? Another hawk?

The shift resolved with me facing a tapestried vista, thread the unfaded tones of spring, but a temple belfry peeking above verdant forest suggested it was pre-dissolution. There was a witch light above my head, turning my vision silver when I blinked. I was posed for her scrutiny.

"What does the goddess mean to you?" asked the queen.

A well of contradictory answers was there for the delving, each sifted out and pored through on the voyage from Fenarin. Refuge. Dependence. Longing. A receptacle for the brightest pieces of my love, mined in the depths of my being, burnished with passion, and returned impartially. I chose the least complex. "I am my Order's mediator, her second mouth and ears."

"That's not the answer to my question."

"The goddess means devotion." I wasn't lying, even if devotion felt more like sodden feathers on my back than wings made for soaring.

"Why?"

Before, I would have said "Whyever not?" and meant it sincerely. The goddess meant devotion; the sea tasted of salt. So simple. I didn't know when my belief had blemished, had only recognised resentment's stain when the queen's magic cocooned god from follower. I required an answer as much for me as for my dance partner. "Because I offered it," I said in the end, "when I needed to know I had something to offer."

"You would have offered devotion to anyone?" asked the queen.

"No." And then—"I'm actually quite discerning."

Amusement creased from her eyes. The storm had broken.

"If I release her, what will you give me in return?"

Did she enquire of all Fenarin or only me? I'd lost who led and who followed to a scattering of smaller sensations, to the press of each finger and thumb, to the brush of our legs—like skimming fresh ocean beneath a fevered sky.

"What do you want?"

We spun out, twined back. No easy capitulation showed in her expression. I tried to define what it was that I saw— curiosity? Admiration? Or was she crafting a dismissal in terms we could never assent to?

"Dance with me tomorrow," she said.

"And then?"

"Ask me again at the end of tomorrow's dance."

Next evening arrived on an exhale and an ebbing tide of questions. The deluge began at dawn's first blush and only stemmed when Alon and I left the consulate for the moon chamber.

What possibly compelled your action? What to read from the queen's response?

Read that we enjoy dancing, was my answer, but the delegates favored interpretations they understood, and the questions eddied without conclusion beyond Alon vowing to weather each full gathering.

Alon posed his question as we paused under a shadow-striped colonnade to breathe before entering the chamber.

"What are you doing, Seri?"

Alon was the least ambiguous of my compatriots, hiding no motive other than to do right by the goddess, an aim to which he dedicated himself quietly and without zealotry. He deserved reassurance. "I'm negotiating with the only authority these people recognise."

"By hanging yourself as bait?" Sharp words bit into my tongue before he shook his head and continued, "No, wait—I'm not implying that. But you understand she's not the goddess?"

Dryly, I said, "I think I'm aware."

He nodded acknowledgement, waved a hand that marked stress in dry discoloration. "I only mean that the goddess acts for others, not herself. Her power is directed by love, but never desire."

"I said as much last night to the queen," I commented,

eyes caught on his hand. Before, I would have prayed for him, but it was his own prayer he needed, one asking nothing other than to be received. I couldn't give him that.

"Then remember your queen doesn't have those constraints. King Harry wasn't a sorcerer until his coronation, and he became a monster. She had magic before it was vested in her. What does that do to a mind? Just think about it, and remember who you deal with. You can't treat her like the goddess."

"*They* treat her like a goddess," I told him. "Removed. Not quite human. I know what she is. That's why I asked her to dance."

"I..." Alon went to smooth a non-existent crease on his sleeve, caught himself, and smiled ruefully. "I worry. Every step feels precarious without the goddess to catch us, and I don't want to fail her."

"It's not all on you." I touched his elbow. His fingers briefly reached to brush mine. "Courage, friend. Let us see what progress can be made this evening." And I strode for the dendrite-patterned doors.

The chamber seethed tonight. Like wasps in a beehive, we were swarmed by buzzing courtiers, silk gowns shimmering with anxious vibration. They pressed for threat and intrigue, in full reversal of our previous cool reception. I knew the queen's entrance from fluttered gasps and breathed a sigh.

"She wears the colors of the goddess," murmured Alon through lips stiff as his jaw.

"Does she suit them?" I craned, resenting his vantage.

"I'd rather decipher their message."

"Her message may be that she suits them."

He dropped a keen glance. "Meant for us or for you?"

That, I dearly wished to know.

She mounted the dais into my line of vision, pausing at the front to regard the court. Regal, displayed, considering. Off. Her gown looked stitched from swathes of sky, cloudless noon at the chest, following her curves down to midnight. Little suns and stars, yellow and white, gave conflict to her light-spurning eyes like buttercups in tar. If the goddess was cut from above, air given shape, the queen was formed from the ore of her land; these colors and motifs were too ephemeral for one so present.

"I'm wrong. They don't flatter her."

"By the goddess, don't share that too loud."

Our words were a low rill to the waterfall of other voices, but it was this moment that she found me in the crowd, passed a challenge in a gaze.

"She knows."

Alon had the look a sailor gets sighting lead depths on the horizon. "Tread with caution, Seri. There aren't centuries of doctrine to glean a queen's moods."

Sound wisdom. How exhilarating it was, though, to dance an uncharted course. "I never blindly followed doctrine," I said, "but I take your warning."

Tonight's music was frenetic, plucked and strummed and fluted with the energy of evening crickets. No controlled burn for these performers; they would slur or trip before the hour matured, but now, the queen and I would blaze across the floor. I left Alon, pushed through whorled courtiers—did the notes move them so, or did they wilfully impede?—to meet her challenge.

The pressure of the room was against me, subtlety blunting in measure with my progress until I was blocked entirely. My obstacle: a rakish man whose beard strained with pearls, excess joviality, and ill-concealed agenda. "There you are! I've been looking for a Fenarin delegate." His arms spread wide, effuse and fencing. "You've the best wine and weavers north of Almir, and the worst trade policies in the Brinik Sea. I've a proposal to change that, one that'll profit us all—and you know, if the right people can be urged to the table, a clever emissary might stand to gain significantly. My agents tell me your wool tariffs—"

The upswell of strings took his remaining words, and I used the opportunity to say, "You speak to the wrong Fenaran, sir. My mandate is purely a spiritual one, though if you'd care to visit the consulate next morning, I'm sure your proposals would meet with interest."

A pause in which he smiled through bristling pearls. "Then you have very little mandate, but all the more reason to consider my offer. Why cling to a sinking vocation when you can ride rising tides to wealth and glory? This could set you up comfortably."

"Comfort of body, perhaps. Call me excessive, but I find I value comfort of mind quite as much."

He was still smiling as he said, "Your obsolete Order won't blight these shores again. Find a new occupation before your people see you for the drain you are. They've no more need for priestesses. You won't change that, no matter how prettily you dance."

"Enough, Arbrique." The queen was beside us, sudden as the snuff of a candle flame. Gravity shifted to make room. Beard tucked to his chest, pearls dimming like morning stars, the man wilted.

"Your Majesty," we both said, mine greeting, his bleat. He curled a bow and scuttled, still bent, into the shrinking wave of peers displaced by the queen's appearance. His words remained, lingering like a sour smell. My eyes compassed to her before he was lost, thrilled in her features.

"You were just over by the dais."

"Yes."

"Clever trick." In the early days of our arrival, stinging from salt residue and laic disdain, we had been invited to watch her pull water to a desiccated well. This was the only time I'd seen her work magic since then, though it clung to her shadow, never lost in bright courtly colors. I liked to think that meant something, a demonstration that she was amenable to our cause. I should have followed with charm, but when I reached for wit, I came up with anxiety. "I didn't join the Order to extort souls for silver," I told her. "I'm no paragon, but I did my best to help people. Those who feared authority too much to invoke it, those whose awe stilted their need. We all—and if not all then most—tried to help people."

Unsaid were the words, *My Order isn't your Order, for all its flaws.* Her courtier likened us to blight. If she thought the same... then he was right: no pretty dancing would resurrect a need for priestesses. I would fail. The identity might chafe, but shucking my duty like poorly fitted vestments would make me something worse, and leave Alon, and every desperate person I'd ever promised succor, to the elements.

The queen contemplated me, head tilted. "I didn't take you as greedy."

"Not materially," I agreed, then amended, "or not more than is common." I craved affection the goddess could never return in kind. That was greed. Perhaps I even harboured greed for the queen.

"And as established, you aren't prone to awe and fear." Now she sounded amused. "I imagine you were a good mediator."

"Thank you." She'd made no judgement on the Order as a whole, but I'd settle for this. "That fellow, Arbrique, does he always weave his hair with pearls?"

"These last years, yes."

"Then he did well from the dissolution?" Dispossessing the Atuevez Order of their land and wealth had filled more than the queen's vacant treasury.

"Very." She looked pleased at my discernment. There were many here who resented our cause. Complex reasons, selfish reasons. My own thoughts were increasingly worm-ridden.

"The goddess for lower wool tariffs?" I tried.

"I think not." But she said it with a ring of humor.

She took my hands, held me at arm's length, cool touch a relief in the oven of bodies and walls retaining the memory of red afternoon.

"No compliment?" she asked. "You told me I looked beautiful before."

"Always. But these aren't your colors. Too airy."

"Hm. A contingent of my advisors counselled I claim her mantle. I told them I wouldn't wear it well."

I tugged her nearer. Music thrummed between us. "Do you want to be a god?"

"Not most of the time." Her teeth flashed a rare grin. "Though they attract interesting devotees."

Pleasure dug roots, and the small fissure in my devotion spread a hair.

Then we danced, and it made us lightning. Through wildfire melody we hewed a serrated line, crooked elbows and knees, split and sparked and struck the boards with our heels. Immediate. Demanding. There was no breath to talk, but our bodies screamed: *Watch me. I am alive.*

At its end, ember-limbed, duty cooled me. A part, a twirl, a final clinch. "What do you ask for the goddess's return?" I asked.

The world was volatile, but her eyes were steady.

"I'm not yet sure of my price." She skimmed a thumb across my knuckles, then dropped my hands. "Tomorrow. Another dance."

"And after, ask you again?"

"If that's what you desire."

I would always desire the goddess free. But what else I desired... needed examining.

Later, in the rooms of the consulate, more questioning: *What does she want from us?* And from Alon: *What does she want from you?* I had my own question, nursed into sunrise, examined for petals and thorns: *What do I want from her?*

The bees descended after morning meal, Arbrique and faction buzzing defense of their queen—and, more importantly, their temple-purloined treasure. Tongues laden with honey, they spilled oblique bribes and threats on the same breath, and though we weren't chased from their shores come evening, I could see the wear on Alon and our cohort.

Another night; a different dance. Pensive music set the pace.

"Why did they choose you?" asked the queen.

"Because I'm close to the goddess and dispensable to current Order workings." I was watching Alon evade courtier drones and slipped her a sideways glance. "Because I deal well with powerful women."

Her laugh could have shifted continents. "Priestesses usually claim humility."

I lifted my shoulders, half apology. "No, that's not a trait one needs to commune with the gods. It requires brashness. Arrogance. A certain disregard of self, perhaps, but not humility."

"The same might be said for communing with a queen. Tell me honestly, would you have me restore her temples here?"

My pulse was near the surface tonight, and I felt it pass into her palm, greedy to be held. "Would you countenance it if I did?"

"I would explain how incredibly impractical I find the endeavor."

"Meaning you can't afford to."

"A *certain disregard of self?* Yes. I inherited a bare-coffered kingdom and a corrupt and incalcitrant branch of the faith. Dissolution wasn't my first choice, but I won't reverse course now. Not for a score of war fleets." The music concluded a phrase, compounding her final sentence.

"We wish her returned where she's wanted and needed, not imposed on your land." This assurance I could extend; discounting a clique of ambitious dissidents, our delegation was too pragmatic to presume otherwise.

The queen nodded concession. "I'll ensure the likes of Arbrique leave you be."

"I wouldn't ask that."

"You don't need to."

No need to ask. No need for prayer. One less wave to batter Alon's rock. It was a perfectly calibrated gift for a goddess devotee. Carve a tenancy in your heart, furnish with joys and sorrows, hang your facets on the walls, set a feast of devotion—this was worship. In return, feel the goddess's warmth, her faith in you. And if you needed more, ask. Always ask, because the channel of her caring, deep and potent as it was, required a bell call to action. I missed the goddess's warmth. But the missing lessened each day, each dance.

It was through dance I spoke my gratitude, bracing and yielding in partnership that transcended hierarchy—my gift to the queen. We mapped constellations across the floor, and I wondered how many nights we would need to leave no grain of wood untrodden. More than we had the funds for. Her focus never left me, though the music dipped.

"What are you thinking?" I said. One song bridged to the next. I held her through it, resetting the night's timer before the last sand fell and I had to ask the question returning me to another's service. I was all too aware of the timer these nights. Soon, our purses would yield no silver. We'd sail then, just as we'd sail if the queen set terms and granted us the goddess.

"I'm considering what might compel a woman who loves to dance as you do to swear to a goddess who can only ever be above it."

"Are you content speculating?"

"Please, enlighten me."

How much of myself to give? Laic questions on the choosing of this path weren't new, but most desired a pious answer, rooted in the virtues of the goddess instead of knotted mortal wants. Most, but not, I suspected, the queen. It wouldn't hurt to show her this. My road to the Order was paved with long-acknowledged flaws and spoke to the benign side of the goddess, far removed from war fleets.

"My family are goldsmiths. Very skilled and respected. I haven't the knack."

"Not everyone does, from my understanding. They rejected you?"

"No. They were good people. They took care of me. I helped with lesser jobs, tried to assist in other ways, but I hadn't the vision to excel."

The unwavering pools of her pupils promised nothing and everything. No shallow reflection ghosted in their darkness. After years of earnest supplicant eyes painting me a flat prelude to the goddess, I could be anything in her vision, and it was rain to scale-parched earth.

"A hard portrait to reconcile," she said.

I shrugged. "They were great, and at best, I was adequate. Everyone saw it. Worse, I envied them."

Skated fingertips soothed and scalded my back. "Is a young girl's envy so bad?"

"A better woman wouldn't resent her family." A better woman might have been worthy of the goddess's undivided love. Or be contented with the portion given. Here I was, bark peeled away, pitted heartwood bare for reading.

She shrugged. "Better women don't match my step. I can't offer the perspective of a better woman. A better queen may have mended her land without provoking invasion. Leave them to their own."

And us to ours? How else to interpret her words? A taste bloomed in my mouth, sweet and intoxicating. I had moved in high circles long enough to know that all rulers had their defects. Some worked to compensate; others, oblivious, let their faults sweep the land like a bridal train through dirt. But even the most aware seldom voiced imperfections. This kinship was vulnerable. Almost... an invitation. Wisdom clashed with want. I was still the goddess's creature, though my soul now sought a different charge in the arms of a flesh and blood partner.

"Perhaps you're right." I tested the ice, committed to a step, saying, "Perhaps I should stop chasing better women and find one better for me."

The queen's quiet was unreadable, accentuated by the swell of the music building to a pivotal phrase, and I wondered: did I overstep? Then her lips twitched, and I comprehended a challenge in her smile.

"Leap," she murmured as the melody crested.

I leapt. Her arms lifted me in flight, strong and solid

and certain. In the cessation of notes between movements, strings humming under stilled fingers, I slid down her body: a beautiful descent. The music resumed, and we embraced to a lazy tempo.

Her breath caressed the shell of my ear. "Now finish your story. What brought you to the goddess?"

"A flood." Tracing my roots felt melancholy after tasting the canopy. "Their shop sits beside a canal. When the great storm passed over and the runoffs failed, we came close to losing everything. I remember asking what I could do. They told me to pray." I spoke in cadence with our swaying, regret blunted by warmth and closeness. "It's likely coincidence that she descended when I joined in entreaty—the whole city was pleading for deliverance. Grey sky tore to show blue, and from the blue knit the goddess, all the beauty of the stars condensed in one being. She saw each of us who'd called her. And when she looked on me, I knew she didn't find my prayer lesser. I think... I think I fell in love right then. Or into an infatuation preceding love. I asked her to save my family's shop. She kissed my cheek"—which prickled in echo, though it was a cool remembrance—"and drank the flood water into herself until the walkways were bare.

"I told my family I was joining the Kafalai Order. And I left."

The queen's hold loosened. Distance worked between us, though there was nothing inattentive in the lines of her face. "And then? Did your ardor grow under her roof?"

"Tenfold," I confessed. "In the temple, I found my awe and respect. I was good at reaching the goddess and good at reaching the supplicants in need of her. I was good at the politics, too. I learned to dance. She gave me a place to find myself. I'll forever love that."

Our contact had reduced to interwoven fingers. A witch light's glow fell through the hollow of our arms, and we viewed each other through its burn.

"You were content in your devotion."

We had reached the crossroads. I could affirm her statement, drop her hands, hope I'd said enough to assure the goddess's return. But the same instinct that spurred my first request to dance kept the truth unspooling.

"I thought I was. I only realized my discontent after news reached us of the Atuevez queen dissolving their Order, after our neighbors declared war to restore the goddess's standing, and the goddess came to the aid of those sailors: when you bound and took her."

There was nothing inscrutable in the intensity of her expression that moment. The sea of courtiers was banished, leaving us and the specter of the goddess and a dance. "What discontent did her absence expose?"

"That my prayers weren't special. I pleaded for her not to cross you, and it weighed nothing more than any other heartfelt prayer. She couldn't ignore a thousand voices crying for help in clear terms. Not for her, and not for me. Unselfish love is all the goddess is capable of. Even my position as mediator, where I found purpose, is only the job of a conduit. I taste more love and devotion in a year than many receive in a lifetime, but only as courier. I love selfishly, and I crave selfish love." In uttering, I'd made it solid, pulling the thorn I'd nursed too long.

We were at rest, music abated.

"The dance has ended," observed the queen.

With the reluctance of surf sinking into the sand, I let her go. No words remained for me but the question.

"What do you ask for the goddess's return?"

She peered at me with all her depths, winter lake melted. "I would ask for you," she said. And added, "Selfishly. But that's not my price. Take her. I can't calm all floods beyond my borders and wish no ruin on those who mean no harm."

She stepped close and kissed me. The feel of her mouth was exquisitely carnal. Under sublime pressure, the plates of my world shifted, entering a new era. I reached to cup her cheek, but she was already drawing away, leaving me on the wasteland of dance floor while she reclaimed her throne. Our talks were done. I took my leave before her courtiers mobbed me.

Sleep was impossible after. I threaded my way through consulate demands of explanation to arrive at Alon's chambers. He was still in his gown, composed and waiting.

"The queen has agreed to the goddess's release," I told him.

Free the grip of turbulent waters, I half expected him to gulp air. Instead, he poured us drinks from a crystal decanter and regarded me with diplomat focus as I took a sip.

"For what price?"

"If I say for me, what will you answer?"

His shoulders stayed square, steadfast. "We sail tomorrow. Without the goddess."

"Why? Bigger concessions have been made, and this concludes our task neatly."

"It would diminish the goddess and our worship. And me."

I rolled the drink over my tongue, but its taste was lost beneath joy, sadness, and gratitude. He was the unselfish complement to the goddess I could never be. "Thank you."

"It's what the goddess would wish."

"Even so, you're a good person and a good friend. But it's not the queen's price. It's mine."

Now he straightened, posture subtly aligning in a way I hadn't seen since leaving Fenarin, a mast emerging from a storm battered but unbroken. He raised his glass, saluted.

"Be careful, Seri," said Alon one final time, and there was a smile in the crosshatching of his face.

Fenarin's delegation sailed the next day, and the following evening I trod through the moon chamber unburdened by divine purpose. The queen tracked my progress through the crowd, fingers curled around the ornate ends of her armrests.

When I was at the foot of the dais, she said, "I don't have any more goddesses stashed away."

"No. Your Majesty, I am Seri, late of the Kafalai Order. I come here to speak with you on a matter quite dear to me."

There were two worlds: one of movement and color and curious whispers, and the other the warmth in her earth-dark eyes. "Oh?"

"Will you dance with me?"

"I will."

Anna Clark is a queer shipyard pipefitter in Cornwall, UK. When not fixing boats or swimming in the sea, she can be found writing speculative fiction on the rocks by the beach. Her fiction has been published in Factor Four Magazine, Gwyllion, Wyldblood.

BERT

Camden Rose

By the time Isabella had put the last piece of athletic tape on her knee, it was too late.

The pink strips glowed green, almost popping off her skin. She tried to peel them off, but the kinesiology tape wouldn't budge. First, putting on the tape felt like being possessed, and now this.

So much for a chill track season.

Her entire room pulsed in the light, her Jonas Brothers posters lighting up like they were zombies. Then, oozing in front of her vanity mirror, appeared a figure. It dripped in dark green slime with three sharp teeth and five hands, one sprouting from one arm and four from the other.

Isabella opened her mouth to scream, but the monster put one of their hands on her mouth while the other shushed her. She breathed in the harsh smell of dirt, graveyards, death.

The monster took their arm away. Isabella wanted to scream, but instead, she shook her head in shock.

"What the fuck?" Her first-ever curse word, not that the monster would know that. "Who—what are you?"

The creature opened their mouth to respond when Isabella heard footsteps coming upstairs. Rough and heavy.

"Everything okay, love?" Mom yelled as she ascended.

Isabella looked between the monster and the door. She wasn't sure how her mother would react to... whatever just appeared in her room. Even if she could get past the slime and the arms and the hands and the teeth, she would have a total freak out from the mess it was making. It would take Isabella toxic amounts of cleaning supplies to get the gunk out of her hot pink fringe rug.

She couldn't tell Mom. Not now, not ever. Maybe, just maybe she could tell her stepdad Jake if he was alone and willing to stand up for her. But never Mom.

Isabella motioned for the thing to get into the closet. "Yeah! All good!" she called. When the beast didn't understand, she put her hands on their chest and pushed as much slime and hands and teeth in as she could.

She was just shutting the doors when Mom poked her head in, wide-framed sunglasses holding her hair up like a headband.

Isabella caught her breath. Held it. Hoped nothing looked amiss. Hoped Mom didn't notice the rug.

"What happened to your knee?" Mom said.

"Nothing." Isabella looked down at the tape. It was no longer glowing. She ripped it off, suppressing a scream of pain.

"Well, when you're done with whatever is going on in here, come downstairs. Jake is setting up for family game night."

Isabella leaned against the door in anguish. "Mom, do I really have to?"

"Yes. You should be grateful that you have a stepdad who wants to spend so much time with you."

Isabella didn't feel grateful. In fact, she felt like Jake was a try-hard. Not that she could tell Mom that. Mom was even harder to talk to than Jake, ironically.

She forced a smile and Mom left, not, of course, without a legendary look of disappointment. Isabella counted to ten after the sound of footsteps disappeared, then opened her closet.

The monster was gone, leaving nothing but her hung-up Hollister tops and flared jeans. She looked for any goo over the clothes, sighed, and closed the doors again.

And that was the day Isabella met Bert.

———◆•◆———

Isabella didn't necessarily want to summon the monster again, but then junior year came. Her knee bothered her still and, more importantly, Stacey wouldn't ask her to prom even though they'd kissed a lot—at the park across the street, under the bleachers, against the lockers at the end of track practice after everyone had left.

In the bright lights of the locker room, Isabella laid the tape in the same pattern. Again, she felt a certain level of possession when she connected the strips. Once the tape was glowing, Isabella's heart rate went up. Maybe this wasn't the best decision.

She took a deep breath. She needed to tell someone. And she'd heard stories about beings making deals, helping others. While she wasn't sure if this kind of monster could do that, she was willing to risk it just in case.

Her love life was on the line after all.

She waited for the creature to appear among the stuffy blue-grey lockers. As the slime grew and grew into hands and teeth and a face, she breathed in the scent of death, debating if it was better than the scent of Abercrombie perfume that permeated the hallways.

"Hey," she said, waving as though that would make this any less awkward. It had taken her weeks to kiss Stacey, and the thought of sharing that information with a stranger made her blush.

The monster turned around, and she noticed now there were two hands on one arm and three on the other.

"Do you talk?" she said, standing up and walking over. She had no closet to push them into this time, but she needed to be brave so that the creature could give her what she wanted.

"Yes," they said, a voice equally baritone and soprano. "I do."

"Good." She held out her hand. "I'm Isabella. Bella for short."

"Berthetandanettatiquities. Bert for short," the monster said. They looked at her hand. Isabella grabbed one of theirs at random and shook it. Bert jumped and yanked their hand away, nursing it like a puppy dog. They glanced up at her. "Don't push me into the darkness again."

Isabella stared at the goo dripping on the tiled floor. At least she didn't have to clean it up this time. There was still a small stain on her rug. Thankfully, her mom never noticed.

"I won't," she said, but Bert glanced back at the lockers in fright, their eyes growing larger and larger as they saw more and more places to be pushed into. "I won't. I swear," she said, holding her hands up. "But only if you help me."

"Help you?" They seemed confused. Isabella opened her mouth to explain, but nothing came out. So, she started pacing.

She had never told anyone that she liked girls. No one. Not even Stacey, though Isabella suspected Stacey knew they weren't just practicing kissing, even if she wouldn't admit it. They were in junior year and neither of them had ever talked about the guys they liked.

If she told her parents she liked girls, Jake might be okay with it, or at least act like he was. Mom would be so shocked she would forget how to speak. That would be even worse than a rug stain.

"..." Bert said, which was technically nothing, but Isabella could feel their eyes following as she turned and walked and turned and walked and turned and walked. Their goo popped like lava.

"What kind of monster are you anyways?" Isabella said, stopping and turning toward them with an accusatory finger. She hoped that by confronting the monster—and how scary they looked—that she'd overcome her own emotional fear.

"I'm not a—"

"I like girls," she blurted. It worked!

"Girls?" Bert tilted their head.

"Girls. Women. Whatever they're called. I like them. Well, one. Stacey. But... she..." Isabella sighed and sat on a bench. "She's too much of a..."

"Girl?" Bert volunteered.

"Yeah, I guess so," she leaned back on the bench, her KT stretching as she did so. Bert's eyes went wide. Isabella leaned forward, her eyes on the slime. "I need you to make her ask me to prom."

"Prom?"

"Yeah, it's a dancing thing." When Bert didn't seem to understand, Isabella sighed and got up. She took two of Bert's hands and danced them around the tiled floor. The slime dripped as Bert moved, so Isabella had to be careful to avoid the slippery spots. "Dancing," she said, letting go of them.

"You want to ask her... to dance."

"No, I want her to ask me."

"Why?"

Isabella sighed and slapped her hands against her legs.

"Ugh, can you do it or not?"

"I don't..."

"Can you?"

"Yes, but..."

So she was right. Bert was that kind of monster.

"But what?" Isabella walked closer, and Bert backed up slowly. She was a good intimidator. That's why she was the track captain.

"But there are rules, a contract."

"For monsters?"

"I'm not a—" Isabella took a step closer, cutting Bert off. The two of them stood there, staring at each other, each of them trying to hide their fear, neither of them exactly succeeding. Her pained scowl faltering, Isabella sighed and then backed off.

"Ugh, fine. I'll just do it myself." She pulled off her tape. Bert disappeared, their goo seeping into the one drain in the entire locker room. Isabella took a deep breath and punched the locker.

It didn't help.

———◆•◆———

A month later, Isabella called Bert in her car. They appeared on top of a McDonald's burger wrapper, goo and slime wrapping around the packaging.

"Hey," Isabella said, her voice weak.

"Hello..." Bert held all their hands up in surrender. Isabella handed them a soda she'd picked up on the way back from school.

"It's Sprite," she said.

"Sprite?" they responded, looking at the plastic straw. "Where are the... wings?"

"Nevermind," she snatched the drink back and took a

sip.

Isabella and Bert sat in silence.

"Did you ask her out?" they said eventually.

"Who?"

"Stacey."

"Oh," she chugged the rest. "Yeah."

Bert's face brightened a bit, somehow. Isabella smiled, then crushed the cup.

"She said no."

Bert deflated. "Oh."

"Yeah," she took a sip, "she thought I was sketchy or whatever. Guess I'm just destined to be alone."

"Oh."

Isabella rolled down her window and dumped the ice out. The sounds of traffic in the distance climbed through the car.

"I'm sorry," Bert said.

"Meh, she was a douchebag anyways."

"Douchebag?"

Isabella sighed and started the car, making Bert jump. They didn't seem to understand anything anymore.

"You—last time you didn't answer my question. Are you a monster?"

"No."

"What are you then?"

"A demon."

Isabella threw her cup in the backseat. She needed to forget Stacey. And, maybe, befriend a demon along the way. That way, when she needed to make a deal, Bert might give her a nicer contract than the typical give-away-your-soul one.

"Have you ever seen a movie?" she said. "I have an in at the local theater. I could tell them you... well, that your youness is just a costume."

And that was the first time Bert ever saw a movie: *Mean Girls* specifically. Their eyes went wide as they tried to process the screen, the sounds, the popcorn kernels that instantly dissolved when they touched Bert's oozing hands–just everything. When they stood up to leave, parts of the movie theater cushion sticking to their slime, Bert was filled with confusing thoughts about high school and a feeling that they may be the first of their kind to ever be with a human like this.

They started hanging out more. Going to other dark venues. Haunted mazes, parks at night, anything where those around might not think twice when they saw the blob of hands and limbs that was Bert.

And, slowly, Isabella felt like they became friends.

They hung out a few times after Isabella left for college, and one time Bert even saw her mom and stepdad from a distance. But, it became hard to maintain summoning a demon when Isabella had a roommate, and even harder once she was swept up in the belongingness. In college, she found her people, the ones who understood her, and she didn't need Bert anymore.

It wasn't until she was home for the summer, and her mom found out she was gay, that she even thought about the demon again.

It wasn't that Isabella had really told her mom, but rather that Mom asked and she couldn't lie her way out of it.

Isabella wasn't sure what she was expecting. Maybe she thought she'd be yelled at, or kicked out of the house or something. Instead, her mom had just put down her fork and said something about how everyone experiments in their youth and Isabella would grow out of it.

That's when Isabella ran upstairs to talk to Bert. Even if it had been a few months, she knew they would understand.

When she tried to recreate the runes on her leg in the middle of her room that felt too small and outdated, she found she barely remembered them and couldn't reach the possession she normally did. Still, she tried and tried until it looked right.

At first, nothing happened, and then there was a dark red glow that she knew wasn't Bert. A monster, ten feet tall and dripping in blood, appeared in her room. Just as it opened its mouth to devour her, she pulled off the tape, and it disappeared, leaving a red stain on her fading, already-stained rug.

"Bert," she cried quietly, "I need you."

Instead, she heard footsteps coming up the stairs. Jake.

"Hey, sweetie, what's going on?" Jake said through the closed door.

"Nothing." She hated that he called her sweetie, as though she was his kid, as though he had been there through everything. As though he'd choose her over Mom.

"Are you sure? You know, you can always talk to me about anything."

"I'm sure!" she yelled and threw a shoe at the door. It bounced off the handle and landed on the fringed rug, right in the pile of blood that used to host a monster. She knew that was immature of her, but she was upset and just wanted to be a kid again.

Instead of going away though, Jake opened the door.

"Well, I'm right here if you ever need to—" Isabella threw her other shoe at him and he took the hint.

Once the door was closed, she cried again, for the life she wanted, the girls she wanted, emptiness of people deciding she couldn't be herself. And, despite how many tears she shed, the blood never left, and her heart never healed.

In many ways, Isabella always knew her mom secretly hated her, and now she had proof.

That was the first time Bert didn't come.

——◆•◆——

Over the course of that first summer, Isabella tried summoning multiple times, especially after each time her mom tried to bring over guys to convert her back, as though that would work.

She tried different patterns and incantations with her KT to get Bert to appear again, but instead she just kept getting monsters of different sizes and concentrations. Most recently, a monster made of toothpicks who just barely managed to nick her face before she'd pulled off the tape.

Looking at herself in her studio mirror, Isabella nursed the cut on her cheek. It kept bleeding, blood dripping down her face like a tear. She wiped it off.

She tried one more rune—one more combination of tape as the rolls slowly dwindled. It was strange being back, without anyone here, feeling trapped between child and adult. Feeling like her mom didn't get her and Bert had disappeared forever. She might be able to be herself in college, but what about at home?

She'd had a taste of what it was like, the belongingness, and now she couldn't go back.

"Bert," she whispered. "Please come back. I don't want to be alone."

There was a knock at the door.

"Bella?" Jake said carefully. Isabella wanted to scream at him, but instead all that came out was a sob. "Is everything okay?"

Isabella ignored him. As usual, he hadn't done anything to stand up for her this whole summer, so he must be on her mom's side.

She needed Bert. Only they would understand. Only they could make Mom forget Isabella's sexuality.

Isabella could do what she'd been planning on doing since she first became friends with the demon. She could cash in her relationship with Bert and get them to give her a contract. Bert could erase her mom's memory of this summer. Maybe she could even stop herself from ever having feelings for women in the first place.

Jake opened the door, hesitated in the doorway, then stepped in. He sat down next to her.

"I know it's hard right now," he started, rubbing his hands together, "but it will get better. And whatever happens, I'm here for you—all parts of you—okay?"

Isabella's tape glowed green and she knew Bert was coming. They were back. They were going to save her from this mess. She stood up, a smile on her face, not caring if Jake saw.

But then, nothing happened.

As Isabella frantically searched everywhere for her friend, Jake shook his head in confusion.

"Can I help?"

"Help me find Bert," she said. She was done with lying.

"Bert?"

"Yeah, they're... they're somewhere..." She opened drawers she knew they couldn't fit in. Searched under the bed. And, after a few seconds, Jake joined her, clearly still a little confused.

As he looked behind a stack of Gwen Stefani and Avril Lavigne CDs, Jake took a glance at his daughter and wiped something from his eye. When he turned back to continue searching for this mysterious Bert in the disc tray of a boombox, Isabella glanced over at him.

Maybe he wasn't as bad as she thought.

They searched for half an hour before Jake cracked a joke, and for some reason, Isabella laughed. He smiled in return, a caring smile that wanted to try.

"I can talk to your mom," he said. "I'm sorry I haven't done so yet."

"She won't understand."

"Maybe not, but she doesn't want you to hurt either. She loves you."

Isabella could barely manage a nod before Jake brought her in for a hug. They stayed like that for a moment, making up for all the years.

Neither of them thought to look outside, where Bert stood, their goo dripping over the bushes. They watched Isabella and Jake and smiled.

Isabella wasn't alone anymore.

Camden Rose is a queer author who loves seeking out magic beneath the everyday world. She can often be found at the ocean's edge taking notes on the local mermaid population. She lives in the Pacific Northwest with her partner, black cat, and collection of books and board games. You can find her online at www.camdenscorner.com.

DELICATE OPERATION

Duane L Herrmann

This old mining scow...
too damned cumbersome,
thruster controls
not sensitive enough.
Matching speed alongside
asteroids – no problem,
within distance
of grappling hooks....
a whole 'nuther matter.
Damn! Not close
enough again!
Shit job of the universe,
here I am!!
Circle 'round
and try again.
Maybe next time
I'll be lucky.

BRADEN HEIGHTS

L.S. Kunz

Jonathan never expected to be living when the town's time capsule got opened, it being a hundred-year time capsule, and he nineteen by the day they buried it. Whenever that box of bygones finally saw daylight again, he should've been planted six feet deep in the family plot alongside Pop, Mother, and Granddad. But nothing was as it should've been.

The town was gone, burnt fiddle to fence post twice over before most everybody finally left back in 2043. The stone marker was still there though. Just as he'd known it would be.

City slickers. Built their houses of little better than sticks and spit. But the monument to the town's time capsule? Granite, of course. Solid granite. Why? Because wouldn't a polished stone look timeless beneath the Braden apple trees. A real testament to the community.

It looked timeless all right. Timeless as a tombstone. And what were the Braden apple trees now? Four torched and twisted husks. A real testament to the community.

Jonathan, leaning on his wheelbarrow, squatted low and brushed soot from the stone marker with a work glove more patches than leather.

The marker was singed black but legible as the day they dedicated it:

Braden Heights
Apple Capital of Utah

Founded June 23, 1999
Time Capsule to be opened at the
Centennial Celebration—June 23, 2099

Apple Capital of Utah. Even in 2053, with every last city slicker dead or driven east where they belonged, the insult still seared like a branding iron.

Jonathan pushed himself back to his feet, stripped off his work gloves, and dropped them in the wheelbarrow beside the rest of his worldly possessions—shovel and pickaxe, of course. Rusty toolbox, picked-over first aid kit, shotgun, half-box of ammo, Margaret Ann's old, battery-operated boombox, a handful of black-market, single-use batteries, and eight jars of home-canned peaches, each wrapped in a white tea towel hand-embroidered with apple blossoms.

Knowing he'd left work undone at the ranch hurt like a pitchfork to the gut, but eight jars of peaches wouldn't last but days, and he had to dig up that time capsule while he still had the energy. Hidden inside that fool box of suburban trinkets was an item more precious than water—an old cassette tape with a recording of Margaret Ann's voice.

Margaret Ann had been just seventeen at the town's dedication. A girl with rosy cheeks, blond curls, and a yolk-yellow sash cinched round her waist. Jonathan couldn't remember the song she sang. Some fool ditty about apples, most like. But the song didn't matter. It was her voice— young, hopeful, sweeter than apple pie.

Jonathan had been nothing more than an angry, young cowpoke back then, with mud on his boots and a plastic sack dripping with fresh cowpats meant for the mayor. But then Margaret Ann had started singing. It was like a bucket of water on a campfire. Could Braden Heights be all bad if an angel like Margaret Ann lived there? Instead of slinging cow pie that day, he'd returned to the ranch determined to win Margaret Ann's hand.

From that day on, he'd done everything he could to deserve a city girl like Margaret Ann. He'd taken over day-to-day operations of the ranch like Pop had always wanted. Within a year, he'd doubled the herd. As the ranches and farms around them transformed into strip malls and tract housing, he'd built Garraway Ranch into an operation to be proud of.

When he'd finally brought Margaret Ann home, it had been to a rambler with all the modern luxuries. And when baby Meg came along, he'd bought her everything a little girl could desire. He'd been a good husband. A good father. Even when the snowpack dried up and revenues ran low, he'd made sure they wanted for nothing.

Jonathan pulled the battered cowboy hat from his head, fanned his face with the brim, and squinted up at the sky. The sun was climbing on toward noon. Already, it radiated like a bonfire on his liver-spotted scalp. If he dug now, odds were his heart would stop before he ever heard Margaret Ann's voice again. And that wouldn't do. The capsule had waited fifty-four years to be opened. It could wait a few hours more.

Scanning the burned-out buildings, Jonathan selected the blackened shell of a hardware store. Its slivers of roof looked sturdy enough to stand a few more hours. He would hunker down there till evening. A breeze would pick up then. That's when he'd dig. No rush. After a lifetime of chores, this was his last task, and he could take as long as he liked.

He steered the wheelbarrow toward the hardware store. Tire crunching on sooty asphalt, he weaved right and left to avoid glints of glass. A flat tire wouldn't be the end of the world—that had already happened. But it would spoil his last hours on this shriveled-up planet.

Braden Heights had been a ghost town for the better part of ten years, and a suburban wasteland for forty-five years before that. But, somehow, Jonathan still saw it as it had been. Before. When the West was cattle and cornstalks as far as a man could see.

The land had been Saul Braden's back then—acres of apple blossoms white as rose-scented snow, and red-ripe fruit as crisp and sweet as a fall breeze. By the time the developers got finished with it, only the four apple trees in the center of town square remained. Four. Pruned and pristine as plastic fruit. Sorry sentinels for the stone marker.

Sure, the children of Braden Heights had lived west of the Rockies, but they hadn't lived in the West. They had only learned about it in school—pioneers and forty-niners, cowboys and coal miners. Even Meg—born and raised on Garraway Ranch—didn't know the West. If she had, maybe she wouldn't have gone vegan to save the planet, then married that computer programmer and moved to Detroit.

He couldn't understand young people today. He had worked hard every day of his life. Never took a vacation. Couldn't recall a single sick day. All he wanted from life was to provide for his family, and America hated him for it. Shouted about animal rights and methane gas and climate change—all while grilling the beef he produced. And the packing corporations? Don't even get him started. Even as beef prices rose, he had gone broke, every year worse than the last, till yesterday when his last heifer died.

In the destroyed hardware store, Jonathan picked his way through burned debris and wedged himself into a shady corner beneath a busted window. The air was stifling as a chicken coop in August. It seared his cracked lips. But at least he was out of the sun.

Around him, melted shelves hulked like mud pots. Looters had toppled a few like dominoes, but there was nothing left to loot. Anything worth taking was long gone—pilfered in hopes it was valuable enough to buy entrance into Detroit or another safe city.

Over the last twenty years, everyone Jonathan had ever cared about had died or migrated east. One by one, he had watched them go—neighbors and friends. Meg. Even Margaret Ann.

He couldn't blame Margaret Ann. Not really. Not when Detroit had so much to offer and he so little. The water was gone. He couldn't say if it was greed or global warming. It didn't matter in the end. First the Great Salt Lake dried up. Then the snowpack failed. Then the groundwater. He had built basins to catch rain water, but you can't catch what doesn't fall.

Then came the toxic winds. The dust storms. The wildfires. Great, sweeping flames that flashed through scrub oak and burnt town and farm alike. The fire of 2041 had claimed the barn and two outbuildings on Garraway Ranch. But he had saved the house and all but a single calf. There was no cause for Meg to leave. He had rebuilt by fall.

After the fire of 2043 took the rambler, Margaret Ann had left too. Called him every kind of pigheaded fool and hitched a ride east with that scoundrel Rick Robinson and his family.

Jonathan kicked the wheelbarrow tire with his scuffed boot and forced his mind back to Margaret Ann's song. The song was all that mattered. He would dig up the capsule and play the recording. He would hear Margaret Ann's voice one last time—sweet and young and full of love, the way she sounded every day of their married life. Till the day she abandoned him.

He must have dozed because he woke with a start. A noise. A footstep? With his hearing half gone, he was more likely to hear the tinnitus in his own ear than danger.

Still.

Quiet as a vole in sawdust, Jonathan pulled the shotgun from the wheelbarrow, rolled onto his knees, and peeked through the broken window. Why would anyone be here? He hadn't seen a soul in more than a year. There was nothing to loot.

Still.

He didn't want to die. Not before he had heard Margaret Ann's voice. He ran his eyes around the square, searching the burnt nooks and charred crannies.

Finally, when he started to turn away, he heard it again.

His eyes darted back to the window. Through cracked shards of glass, he saw a shadow move. Across the square in the shell of the grocery store.

Jonathan held his breath. Seconds ticked by like drumbeats. Like waiting on a cow to calve. He raised the shotgun to the window and watched.

The shadow loomed large and materialized into a mangy pit bull. Its black fur dusty. A patch of white on its chest spotted red with blood. Abandoned when its owner fled east, no doubt. A length of chain still dragged at its neck like a noose. Thick saliva dangled from the corners of its panting mouth, and a tangle of rusty barbed wire crippled its haunch.

The pit bull sniffed the ground, hobbled a few steps, and licked its paw. With each step, the twisted barbed wire cut deeper into the dog's flesh.

Jonathan must have moved because the pit bull's tail tensed, its ears stood on end, and its dull eyes hardened into amber and darted toward the hardware store, boring through the warped glass into Jonathan's cataract gaze. Jonathan held his breath. Finally, the pit bull turned and limped toward the stone marker.

Jonathan melted back to the ground. A hurt dog was a dangerous dog. By nightfall, it would have died or moved on. It was nothing to him.

But he could still hear the staccato scrape of the barbed wire. He could barely hear anything anymore, but he could hear that dog's misery.

He covered his ears.

Scrape. Scrape.

Such a brave dog. Tangled in barbed wire, bearing down on death, but it didn't complain. Didn't even whimper.

Jonathan couldn't take it. He pushed himself to his feet, pulled wire cutters from his toolbox and, after a moment's thought, grabbed the first aid kit and canteen as well.

The dog had reached the stone marker and was sniffing the inscription.

When Jonathan stepped into the street, the dog tensed so hard it shook. A low growl rumbled in its throat. It faced Jonathan, ears angled, amber eyes narrowed to mean slits.

Jonathan shifted sideways and focused his gaze on the stone marker. He kept his hands at his side and spoke in a voice low but firm as if to a skittish horse.

"It's all right, boy. I'm not gonna hurt you."

He took a slow step forward.

The dog braced and growled, low and raspy at the back of its throat.

Jonathan took another step.

The dog paced and bared its teeth.

Jonathan narrated his approach. His words low and steady. "I know. They abandoned you, didn't they? Headed east and left you behind? Don't you worry. You'll show them. You're a fighter. We just need to pull that wire away."

The dog splayed its forepaws and released a loud, vicious volley of barks.

Jonathan waited.

The barking subsided to a high-pitched whine.

Jonathan took another step.

The dog cowered back on its haunches, ears flattened against its scalp, trembling.

Jonathan kept talking. Calm and confident. As if nothing was wrong.

Finally, he reached the dog's side. Narrating each step, he knelt, slipped the wire cutters around a length of barbed wire, and squeezed till the rusty wire snapped in two.

The dog started as if to flee but stayed put. Its body rigid as firewood.

Jonathan cut another length of wire and worked it away. Then another and another till the dog was free, its wounds fiery red and oozing.

By now, the dog was limp. Jonathan tilted the dog's head, slipped the chain from the dog's neck, and dropped it. The dog nipped at Jonathan's hand but didn't break the skin.

Jonathan treated the dog's wounds and wrapped them with gauze, gave the dog a long drink from his canteen, and shuffled back to the hardware store.

The sun was blazing. He needed a drag of water too and some rest.

But as he sank down in the shade his eye fell on the eight jars of peaches. Each in their own clean, white tea cloth. The last of Margaret Ann's bottled bounty. Once jars of fruit and vegetables fresh from their garden had filled the cellar. Now, these were the only jars left. Saved till last because they tasted most like sweet memories of Margaret Ann.

He reached for a jar, hesitated, and reached again. With the tea towel removed, the glass was cool and smooth against his hot, cracked skin. Almost like holding Margaret Ann's hand. He lifted the jar into a sliver of sunlight and admired its glistening, apricot-gold jewels. Finally, he hobbled back into the sun, crossed the cracked asphalt, twisted the jar open with a pop, and set the contents before the half-panting, half-dozing dog.

Letting go of the jar hurt like tearing a piece of himself away.

He turned his back on the golden syrup, returned to the shade of the burnt-out hardware store, and fell asleep beneath the busted window.

When he woke, the dog was beside him, its boxy head resting in his lap, its gauze-wrapped legs twitching in sleep. The peach jar at its feet, licked clean.

Jonathan smiled. His lips split and cracked like an old rubber band.

He patted the dog's head and ran his hand down the dog's back. Stopped. Backtracked. The dog was bone thin, of course. But there was something else.

He pushed the fur aside. Scars. Old. New. Everywhere. Not just abandoned then. Abused and abandoned.

Jonathan liked the weight of the dog's head on his leg. But he couldn't lead the dog on. The dog would live for days yet, years maybe. But Braden Heights was Jonathan's last stop.

He scooted away and let the dog's head droop to the cracked, sooty floor.

Jonathan dozed again and when he woke a second time the dog's head was back in his lap. The dog was awake this time too, staring up at him with wide, ripe-wheat eyes.

Jonathan pushed the dog's head away. "Off with you

now."

Using the wheelbarrow for support, Jonathan pressed himself to his feet. The dog struggled up beside him, tail wagging.

Jonathan peered through the cracked window. The sun had dipped toward the distant mountain peaks. It was time.

He wrapped the empty glass jar in its tea towel, returned it to the wheelbarrow beside the seven remaining jars, and pushed the wheelbarrow out into the street.

The dog limped behind, close at Jonathan's heels.

Jonathan shrugged. "Come if you like. But you best stay out of my way. I've work to do."

Back at the stone marker, Jonathan parked the wheelbarrow and lifted the pickaxe. It felt heavy as an anvil. When he took a swing, the blade barely made a dent. The soil was as compact as concrete. He took another swing. A few clods of dirt broke away. He wiped his brow, retrieved his work gloves, and started in earnest.

Jonathan threw all his strength into the task. Swing after swing till the soil loosened. When he switched from pickax to shovel, the dog scooted forward and helped.

When the hole was big enough to sit in, dog and man sat down and shared a jar of peaches. The dog's tongue lolled. Its tail wagged. Jonathan let it lick the jar clean before he wrapped the jar back in its tea towel and returned it to the wheelbarrow.

After another hour, the shovel hit something solid.

Shoulders sore and hip acting up, Jonathan worked his way down to his knees and cleared the dirt away. Pointy metal. The corner of a box.

He whooped. The sound of joy disintegrated into the rust-orange sunset. The dog flinched but wagged its tail. Jonathan laughed. "We found it, boy. Come on."

Redoubling their efforts, dog and man dug around the capsule till it wiggled. Grasping the box with both hands, Jonathan rocked it back and forth till it broke free.

Tumbling onto his rump, Jonathan displayed the steel box like lost treasure. The dog cocked its head and sniffed the box.

Jonathan laughed. "I know. It doesn't look like much. But it's everything. Trust me."

Sitting on the stone marker, Jonathan worked at the rusty hinges till the lid popped off.

The capsule was stuffed full.

Jonathan looked around for a clean spot and settled on the stone marker. After wiping the granite slab with his sleeve, he upended the capsule and poured its contents out. Trash from the nineteen-nineties toppled onto the engraved stone.

Stripping off his work gloves, Jonathan picked through the contents but didn't see the cassette tape. Where was it? He wanted to rummage, shove the garbage out of the way till he found the gold he was seeking, but he forced himself to work slowly. The tape would be fragile after fifty-three years underground.

Finally, there was nothing left on the stone but a freezer baggie full of what? Rotten rice? Jonathan leaned in. Seeds. A plastic baggie of seeds. The baggie itself was a novelty. A wrinkled relic of a disposable past. When he grasped it, it crinkled between his fingers and threatened to split. But Jonathan didn't care about the baggie. He pushed it aside. Underneath, brittle but intact, was what he had come for. Margaret Ann's cassette tape.

Tears sprung to his eyes when he recognized Margaret Ann's loopy script. Her handwriting hadn't changed. Why had she? Jonathan wiped the tears away and, using both hands, lifted the cassette from the stone as gently as he had lifted Meg for the first time.

Cradling the cassette in his palm, Jonathan retrieved the boombox from the wheelbarrow and set it on the ground. Margaret Ann had kept the boombox all these years. Listened to it even as he had bought her new, better electronics. Danced to it as she cleaned the house. Turned the volume up if Meg complained the music was outdated. Bought batteries on the black market to keep it running. Repaired it more than once. Chose it among all her treasures to save when the rambler burned. But then left it behind when she walked away from Garraway Ranch.

Jonathan pressed the eject button, and the cassette door popped open. Sliding the cassette in, he pushed the door closed again till it clicked. Finger trembling, he pressed play.

The machine whirred and static popped in the speakers, but no music came. Jonathan checked the volume. It was fine. As gently as he could, he pressed rewind. The machine jumped to life and let out a squeal, rewinding the tape so fast it nearly made his heart stop.

Finally, the player clicked off. Once more, Jonathan pressed play. This time, after a brief silence, he heard clapping and cheering and chattering voices. When a guitar twanged, the crowd kept talking. But when a voice joined the guitar, all other sounds fell away. Soon Jonathan was alone with the sweet, clear voice of his Margaret Ann.

When I find him, he'll be the apple of my eye.
He'll be my sunshine. He'll be my ever-loving sky.
When I find him, I'll stay with him till I die.
I'll be his girl. He'll be my guy.

The chorus gave way to another verse, but Jonathan didn't hear it. The bright-eyed girl with the yellow sash stood on stage with her guitar. His Margaret Ann. When he had seen her that day, he had known she was everything. He had worked his fingers raw to give her everything she deserved, but she had left anyway. She hadn't stayed with him. Not in the end.

When I find him, it's sure I'll know him by the spark.
We'll have picnics in the park.
We'll take long walks in the dark.

The song turned back to the chorus, and Jonathan's mind turned back time. In the early years, he and Margaret Ann had gone on lots of picnics. Lots of walks—in the dark, in the rain, in the orange glow of sunset. But that had been long ago. Before chores and bills and baby Meg. Eventually, they had stopped frittering their precious time away.

Or had they?

Margaret Ann had asked on occasion. She had packed picnics too. He remembered now. Nights he came home late when dinner hadn't been waiting in the oven but in a basket. How long had it been since he had seen that basket? He couldn't remember.

The strum of guitar died away. Margaret Ann's voice disappeared. After a breath, there was loud, long applause. Someone called out Margaret Ann's name. Someone else whistled. Eventually, even the applause died away, and Jonathan was alone. Again.

But he wasn't. The dog nudged Jonathan's arm. Jonathan patted the dog's head. The dog whined.

"What? Want to hear it again?"

The dog tilted its head.

Jonathan nodded. "Me too."

Gently, he pressed rewind and cringed at the heart-stopping squeal. When the player clicked off, he pressed play and let the song wash over him. The dog lowered its head to Jonathan's lap, and the two listened together.

When the song gave way to applause, Jonathan pressed stop. He patted the dog's head. It was time.

He wanted to shoo the dog away, retrieve the shotgun, end life the way he had lived it—on his own terms.

But something stopped his hand. Something gnawing the pit of his stomach. Something wrong that had to be put right. What?

Jonathan took up the chain that had served as the dog's collar and ran his fingers along it. When he got to the end of the chain, his fingers stopped. The last link was stretched and twisted. Broken. The dog hadn't been abandoned. It had run away. It must have taken weeks, months, to strain against the chain till it finally broke.

Jonathan stroked the dog's head.

"It must've been real bad for a loyal pup like you to run away."

Jonathan's hand stopped rubbing the dog's fur.

The dog whined.

But Jonathan didn't hear. He was looking east.

"It must've been real bad."

Jonathan sat up so suddenly the dog scrambled back and cocked its head.

Jonathan laughed. "That's right. Time to get a move on. Detroit's a long way off, and we've only got six jars of peaches left thanks to you, you greedy mutt."

Jonathan reached for the wheelbarrow to push himself to his feet, but stopped. What was he thinking? He couldn't go to Detroit. They wouldn't let him in. He didn't have anything to offer but a beat-up dog and an old boombox.

Jonathan's hand twitched. There was something, wasn't there? He looked at the debris from the time capsule scattered on the ground. There it was. A baggie of seeds. Gently, he pulled the baggie open and peered inside. Apple seeds from Saul Braden's orchard. Thousands of seeds. Hard and round and firm. Young people didn't want beef anymore. But they wanted fruit. People would always want fruit.

They'd let in an old man if he brought an orchard with him, wouldn't they? He could find Margaret Ann, and Meg, and the computer programmer. He could meet little Annie. She must be ten now, maybe eleven. It wasn't too late. People still went on walks in Detroit. Didn't they? They must. What was the point if they couldn't go on walks?

The pit bull by his side, Jonathan pushed himself to his feet, dusted the ash from his pants, and turned east.

L.S. Kunz lives with her husband in the rolling foothills of northern Utah. She has been published in Ellery Queen Mystery Magazine *and* Utah's Best Poetry & Prose 2023, *and has received awards for her short and middle grade fiction. When she isn't writing, she enjoys hiking, camping, gardening, running, watching wild critters in her backyard, and reading almost anything she can get her hands on.*

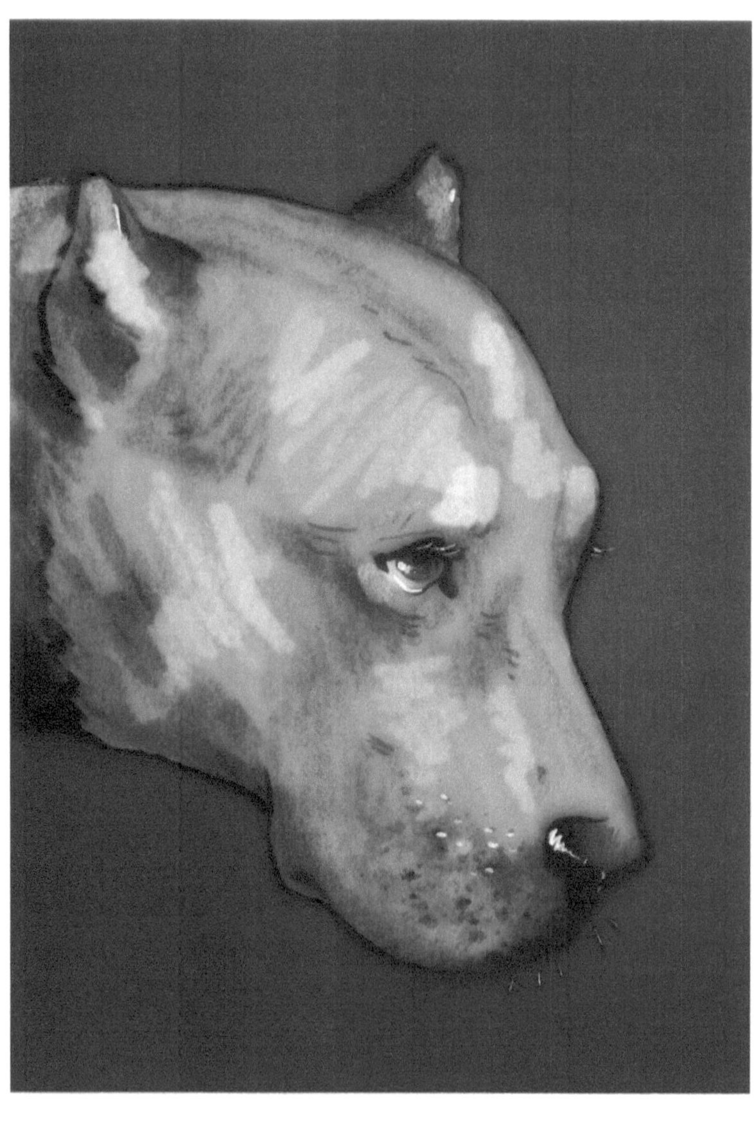

The Wine of Communion

Hardy Coleman

Remember that Friday night a coupla weeks back it got down to seventeen below? Well anyway, that's the last I seen of Jesus. Had a half-empty bottle of Lizard Piss with him that he stuck into the snow, did a little dance around it, mumbled a few hallelujahs and when he pulled it out, tasted just like vintage M. D. 20/20. Only better, if you can believe that. One healthy swig and it felt like you'd swallowed a propane heater.

"This swill is Goddamn miraculous!" I said.

He just chuckled and blew his big red nose.

So we found some scrap wood and built a fire there by the Mississippi, shot the breeze about the best spots to fly a sign, how it's most generally the folks driving rusted-out shitmobiles that'll toss you a dollar or a hand fulla change. Ain't never them bastards in their B. M. W.'s with the windows rolled up tight. Talked about women and lawmen. It's kinda weird, you know? Speak of the Devil, then up show the cops.

"Oh shit, not this again," said Jesus, then he took off running. I figured he musta knowed somethin I didn't, so I done the same. Looking back, I reckon I assumed that dude would posses Olympic speed but then, he's old, ya know? And I shoulda listened cause he's always yammering about where those government boys drove them nails through his feet. "Hell yeah, Skunk, I used to be a wide receiver. Could scorch both you and your pet cheetah on a post pattern seven days a week, even if I was schnockered. Course, that was back before the fucking nails."

So like I was sayin, we was high-tailing it across the ice but the cops were gaining on account of them holes in his feet and also, he was pretty well piss-faced. Now me, I don't particularly mind a night on the county's expense. (At least it's dry and warm.) But Jesus, get him rolling and he can tell you a few stories about some of the cells he's slept it off in. Suffice it to say, he ain't in no hurry to go back.

But we come up to this patch in the middle where the water tends to get all bubbly and runs fast and right then his feet gave out. I mean, gent just went down on his knees like he's prayin to his old man or somethin. These two gumshoes ain't more'n fifteen, twenty steps behind us shouting crap like, "Stop, in the name of the law!" and "Up against the wall, motherfucker!" and "Go ahead, make my day!" And by the sound of it, they meant business, too.

What the hell am I gonna do? He ain't too heavy, as in; That's what you get on a diet of homemade wine. So I grabbed him under his smelly armpits and threw him over my shoulder like he's a sack of dirty hymnals and off we went, skating over the water on nothing but faith and fumes. The ice was real thin, you could see right down to the bottom and let me tell ya, there's some ugly-ass creatures swimming around down there gnashing their teeth. And oh man, what teeth!

But skate we did! Then just about the time we'd made it across and we was fixin to head into the woods, them two coppers pull out their roscoes and shout, "Gigs up, you low- life skeezicks! Hands in the air or you're sleeping at the morgue tonight!"

Hey! Wadn't our fault that the ice was flimsy. Wadn't

our fault them two fuzz roaches was overly fond of dough nuts.

I turned when they hollered and threw my mitts in the air, dropping old Jesus like stolen loot. "Don't shoot!" I shouted back.

But they did shoot, them stupid flatfoots. Guess they figured a couple lushes for target practice wadn't nothin more'n good, clean fun. However, right as they was squeezing off their rounds; right as they was planning what to tell their cronies back at Dunkin D's what they done to them two winos on the river, the ice broke. I felt the heat of a bullet part my hair and heard screaming sounded the same as in that movie, *Jaws*, when the shark's munching down his breakfast. Then it got all quiet and peaceful there on top of the water.

"That was close, man," I said, then looked down at my buddy. "Crap! He's got hisself hit." Ain't nothing more'n a pile of rags and bones, that long hippie hair of his lookin dark as his blood in the moonlight. Went down to sitting and gathered him up in my arms like his momma woulda. "You fuckin pigs!" I yelled. "Can't you see he didn't mean no harm?" And I started to cry right there, my two butt cheeks stuck to the ice. Didn't give a rat's patoot if anybody seen it or went and told the news lady. Friends is kinda rare in my social echelon, and I'd just lost a good one.

⁕

But that ain't the end of the story.

Few days later I was cheating my way through a game of solitaire in the county's petty misdemeanor hotel. It had been a slow night for business: Wadn't nobody else been arrested except old Toothless Larry, and he was passed out, snoring like a congested hog. Then I heard a steel door clang and the rattling of keys. It was Officer Friendly come to set me free.

"Morning, Skunk," he chimed, a little too bouncy. "Time to rise and shine!"

"I need a bloody Mary first."

"We're not that kind of hotel," he replied.

"Cup of coffee?"

"O. K. Cup of coffee." He led me down the hall to receiving and poured me a cup. "Saw your friend on Sunday."

"My friend?"

"Yeah. Your main man, Jesus."

"Piss off, lawman!" This was gettin me angry. "Your people shot him down last Friday."

Talk about shit-for-brains ... "Well you know, that's the wonderful thing about this great nation we live in." He just kept right on smilin. "Capitalism, Skunk! That's where it's at."

"What kinda crap you talkin?"

"You just can't keep a good man down." Officer Friendly stood there like I was supposed to figure it out. Stupid as he is, still, I guess he could tell by my face that I wadn't getting it. "He's back. Jesus is back!"

I shoved my fist in his mug. "I told ya piss off once already! Don't toy with me, asshole."

He stumbled backwards, held his hands up in front of hisself. "I'm not! I've got proof."

"Go on."

He reached into his blue coat and pulled out a flask. Unscrewed the cap, offered it to me. "Here, give this a snort."

I musta looked pretty skeptical.

"You want proof. This is the proof."

I took a mouthful. Sure enough, it was the proof ... High proof stuff. Good old M. D. 20/20 with a propane chaser. I just grinned and handed it back.

"What did I tell you?" Officer Friendly chuckled. He knocked one back, but instead of the pleasure of a good belt, his expression turned to confusion. He eyed the flask, then took another swig. Then he spat it out; spewed it all over my face.

Now I been drinkin various and sundry liquid refreshments for quite a little while. Some folks might even call me a professional imbiber. I know my fluids.

"This IS NOT what he gave me!" Friendly was real hot under the collar. "I told him if he'd keep me supplied with that grade A wine he makes, that I wouldn't haul him in." He dumped the contents out onto the floor. PURE, CLEAR WATER. "Damn! I already collected money from half the guys on vice squad for advance orders."

Right then, I seen it clear as a glass of corn liquor. He always was a sly bastard, that Jesus. My grin turned into a big, gap-tooth smile. "Thanks for the drink, Officer. But I really gotta be rollin along. I hear H2O is good for ya." Nodded my head at the puddle on the concrete floor. "Ya shouldn't oughta waste it."

Then I picked up my belt and shoelaces at the admissions desk and walked on out into the bright, cold morning. Headed towards the river, lookin for an old friend and a shot of holy water.

Leonard Hardison Coleman—"Hardy"—was born October 29th, 1952.

Descended from a long line of medical doctors, he felt he was expected to follow in those footsteps, but telling stories and writing poetry were the two activities that fueled him for his entire life. After two years at Simpson College and the University of Iowa, where he befriended author Denis Johnson, Hardy turned away from formal education. He moved back to Clear Lake, Iowa, where many of his family lived, before moving to Minneapolis, where he truly belonged.

In Minneapolis, he found work in many different fields. First, at a nursing home, where he met his first wife. Then as a cook at the Mud Pie, where he once took an order from Bianca Jagger and also served the B-52's. He owned a moving company and his last full-time occupation, before the pandemic, was as a taxi driver. He and his cab were sometimes featured in music videos, including one by Nathaniel Rateliff and the Night Sweats, where he can be seen dancing in the arms of his partner, Patricia. He and Patricia are also featured in the book, *American Dreams*, by Ian Brown.

All these experiences, plus raising his three children, fueled his poetry, plays, and short stories.

His children's book, *Game Day*, was published by Moonfire Publishing in 2022, and he was thrilled to read it to many audiences in schools and bookstores in Iowa and Minnesota. Tapes of Hardy's poetry readings are up on YouTube and harbored in publications like *Does It Have Pockets?* and *The Ravens Perch*, and some of his poems are featured in the anthology *The Road by Heart: Poems of Fatherhood*, edited by Greg Watson and Richard Broderick.

Blessed with "green thumbs—and fingers" his wild and

beautiful gardens in South Minneapolis—where much is wild and often not beautiful—have gathered praise from neighbors and passersby, not to mention the assumed appreciation of the butterflies and bees.

Hardy passed away on March 26th, 2024, shortly before an email from *Baubles From Bones* landed in his inbox, accepting "The Wine of Communion" for publication. We were heartbroken when Patricia responded to let us know of his passing. He put his heart into every word, and you can tell. We are honored to have a piece of him here in our magazine.

—Elyse Leskovic, with help from Patricia Enger.

Photo of Hardy Coleman by Mercies May

WANDERING STAR

Sarena Ulibarri

Iva aimed her telescope in the opposite direction of the village's sparkling fireworks, waiting for the sun to fully set so she could track the faint blur that had been growing brighter over the last few nights. The mystery and quiet melody of the comet wandering through the constellation of the Separated Lovers excited her much more than the villagers' drunken merriment. Especially on a holiday that only reminded Iva of all she'd lost, of the culture and family she could never regain.

As she tinkered with the telescope's eyepiece, something whooshed past, much closer and more colorful than any star. Iva's heart sped up, hope blooming.

"Lotkia," she whispered, the name nearly a song on her lips. She couldn't see who steered the green and purple paraglider, but who else ever arrived in the village this way? Iva abandoned the telescope and ran, leaping over flowers and dodging mossy boulders, guessing where her beloved friend was likely to land.

Lotkia passed overhead, pulling at ropes and handles. She veered uncomfortably close to the trees, but Iva knew she could attune with the winds, ask them to carry her wherever she wanted.

Once she landed, Iva stopped a dozen feet away and watched Lotkia unstrap herself from the deflating parachute and pull a lever to retract the fan blades into a pouch on her back. Then their eyes met, and Lotkia dropped all her equipment with a sly smile. Iva stood still, letting Lotkia come to her.

"Did the winds tell you I was coming?"

The songs of the air were too transient, too chaotic for Iva. She preferred the stability and subtle hum of the stars, and the faraway planets she could only see through her telescope.

"My heart told me," Iva answered. Lotkia pulled her into a kiss that melted away all the time they'd spent apart.

Lotkia touched the streak of silver among the rest of Iva's dark hair. It wasn't there the last time Lotkia visited.

"You should come to the city; it will keep you younger."

"Maybe so," Iva said. Lotkia's dark skin was still perfectly smooth, not a wrinkle visible around her green eyes, her hair as shiny black as always. Lotkia snaked an arm around Iva's shoulders, guiding her back toward the paraglider. Together they folded and packed it into the pouch.

"How is your father?" Lotkia asked.

Iva paused, a knot half-tied. "He... passed."

"Just recently?"

"Almost a year ago," Iva admitted.

Lotkia finished securing the pouch. "Why didn't you tell me?"

It had been two years since Lotkia visited the village, but Iva could have written. She drew lines in the loose dirt with her fingertip, refusing to meet Lotkia's gaze.

"I didn't want to spread the grief. And...if I wrote it down, it would become too real. This way, at least you still lived in a world where he was alive."

Lotkia kissed Iva's forehead. "I'll burn my herbs for him tonight at the solstice." Iva sighed, and Lotkia gently pinched her arm. "You were going to skip it again, weren't you?"

Indeed, she was. Summer solstice had been her favorite holiday when they were children, back on their island home, before stone magic gone wrong had awakened the dormant volcano and turned the island paradise of Nor into a fiery disaster zone. The villagers only celebrated as an excuse to feast, drink, and dance, with little regard for connecting to the planetary rhythms. But Lotkia still loved it, and Iva loved Lotkia.

"Let me take down my telescope," Iva said.

⬥•⬥

A caravan had pulled up to the village earlier that day, bringing nomadic performers who traveled between the two continents, trading tricks and entertainment for food and supplies. They added an extra flair to the solstice, breathing fire and dancing with swords, doing back handsprings across the tables and juggling fruits.

After the feast, Iva helped clean the tables while everyone else, including Lotkia, wandered out to the celebration grounds to set off fireworks. Iva found her later in a small group clustered around a bonfire. Lotkia sat close to a man—one of the performers, the firebreather. One of her hands clutched a flask, the other rested on his thigh. Iva fought down a surge of jealousy, and put on a smile as she strode toward them.

Lotkia spotted Iva and stood, unsteady on her feet. Clearly, she'd had too much of whatever the flask held. She clasped Iva's arm and drew her toward the fire.

"This is Sev. He's Norian. He's like us!"

Iva recognized Sev as the type of man that women often found appealing. Skin a little darker than Lotkia's, thick dreadlocks that brushed broad, muscled shoulders.

His teeth were straight and white, and his cheeks dimpled when he smiled. Iva could appreciate his beauty, but men never sparked any desire in her. Lotkia, on the other hand, seemed enraptured. Iva intentionally sat in between them.

"You're a survivor?" Iva asked.

"I was very young," he said. "I don't remember much."

"Too bad," Iva said. "Nor was a place to remember. But you can hear the songs?"

In answer, Sev caught a curl of the bonfire without burning his hand. He guided the fire to grow, then change into the shape of a beautiful woman. With a clap of his palms, the fire disappeared. "It's just tricks and games, anymore," he said.

Lotkia leaned across Iva toward Sev. "Show me more tricks and games."

Sev stood, taking Lotkia's hand and pulling her up with him. "Come back to camp with us."

"Oh no," Iva said. She pushed between them and draped Lotkia's arm over her shoulder. "It's time for us to go home."

After a little more cajoling, Iva led Lotkia away from the bonfires and firebreathers. The usual constellations decorated the sky, but the faint blur she'd spotted was not quite bright enough to see without her telescope.

"I want to show you something," Iva said once they reached her cabin. She set up her telescope at the bedroom window and found the comet, a little clearer now than the night before.

Lotkia stumbled and her hand hit the telescope, knocking it off of its target.

Iva patiently guided the scope back to the right part of the sky, but Lotkia was unimpressed by the wandering star. She dropped onto the bed with a dramatic sigh.

"Why do you waste your time with stars?"

"I hear their songs, just like you hear the winds'."

"But the wind is useful," Lotkia said. "What good are the songs of something so far away?"

"Have you ever heard the song of our whole planet?" At Lotkia's baffled look, Iva continued, "You can't hear the song of our own planet because all we can hear is the voice of each stream or mountain, drowning out everything around it. But when you're far enough away, the song of a whole planet creates a harmonious chorus, all those songs blending together into something that's more than the sum of its parts."

"But you can't do anything with that."

Attuned with the wind, Lotkia could ask them to change direction, to speed up or slow down. Those who attuned with plants and trees could ask them to grow faster, or in a particular configuration, like the great castles of Nor, which had been formed from living wood.

"Maybe I could," Iva said. She flopped onto the bed and brushed a strand of pitch-dark hair out of Lotkia's face. "Every earthquake or aurora on our planet could be the whisper of someone listening from another star. Maybe the very rotation of this planet was decided by faraway voices."

"Mmm," Lotkia said, but she had buried her face in Iva's neck, not listening anymore.

Iva wrapped her arm around Lotkia, and the songs of the stars disappeared beneath the rhythm of their heartbeats, ticking away the shortest night of the year.

⚬•⚬

When Iva woke the next morning, Lotkia was already hooking her pouch onto her back. She rolled over in bed and rested her chin on stacked hands, watching Lotkia fuss with the tangled straps.

Iva bit back all the questions she wanted to ask: Why couldn't she stay longer? When would she be back? Might she visit more often? She'd learned long ago that these questions only irritated Lotkia, and the answers, when she would give them, were never accurate. Lotkia was as unpredictable as the winds she attuned with, as ephemeral as a passing breeze.

Iva dressed and followed Lotkia to the edge of the cliff.

"Will the winds carry you to the top?" Iva stared out across the foggy bay to the massive cliffs of the northern continent, barely visible on the horizon.

"No, it's too high." Lotkia tenderly touched Iva's cheek. "Come to Kezik with me. We can hike down to the fishing hamlet instead, and take the train that climbs to the top. Together."

Iva shook her head, not bothering to offer the usual excuses.

They kissed once more, and then Lotkia backed up, holding onto Iva's fingers until the last second. Iva crept to the edge and watched her fall, the purple and green paraglider puffing out just before she disappeared into the clouds below.

⸻ ❦ ⸻

The anniversary of her father's death arrived. The villagers believed the soul lingered near the body for a whole year, so the one-year ritual was even more significant than the funeral. They all claimed they wanted to support Iva in her grief, and yet Iva found herself sitting on the Griever's Stone by herself. Even the groundskeeper who prepared her father's body had apologized and told her they were too busy to stay.

"It's nothing against you or your father, you know?"

"Of course," Iva replied with a tight smile.

The village had welcomed the Norian refugees after the disaster that destroyed the island. Iva's father had held her hand the entire long hike from the southern shore, but told her only "hush" each time she asked where her mother was. She remembered the kind smiles of the villagers who took them in, the bland food that had tasted like a miracle. A few dozen Norians had made their home here during Iva's childhood, but as she stared at the cairn covering her father's body, Iva appreciated that now she was the only one left.

Anger flared through her. She twisted the mourner's veil in her hands, then yanked it off and tore the thin fabric in half. She'd honored the villagers' death traditions, yet they hadn't even bothered to show up. She and her father had never truly been a part of this village; these customs had never been their own. Now Iva was the only one here who remembered the tropical fruits of Nor, the only one who could hear the songs of the mountains and trees and rivers. All of those vibrations rushed in on her now, a loud cacophony of stone, plant, water, and wind. Everything she usually blocked out in favor of the subtle sounds of the stars.

Come to Kezik, Lotkia had pleaded, this time and every time she'd visited for years. Iva had always resisted, not willing to lose a second home. But there were more Norians in Kezik. Lotkia was in Kezik. Despite the cold weather and crowded streets, the city might be more like home than the village had ever been.

———————◆•◆———————

At sunrise, without saying goodbye to a single person in the village, Iva left the door to her cabin wide open and started down the cliffside trail. The path wound past the ossuary, but Iva resisted a last look at her father's cairn. She was looking forward now, not back.

Fog thickened as she descended, obscuring both the sun and the fishing hamlet below. One misstep on a steep part of the trail sent her tumbling off the path, somersaulting until she crashed against a boulder. She scrambled to check the telescope. It was intact, no cracks or scratches on the lenses. She breathed a sigh of relief.

Her ankle, on the other hand, was in much worse shape. Iva freed her boot laces to lessen the constriction. Pain flooded in. Her whole foot swelled, the skin red and mottled. She wasn't sure she could stand, much less make the rest of this journey.

"Need a hand, love?" In her pain and confusion, Iva thought for a moment that it was Lotkia. But the accent was all wrong, the voice higher pitched.

Fog swirled around a man and woman wearing loose knit clothes, each carrying a basket full of a fruit that grew on vines along the cliff. They were olive-skinned, with silver hoops in their ears and noses.

"I don't think I can walk."

The woman handed her basket to the man and tied her long brown hair into a loose bun as she navigated the uneven ground to reach Iva. "Little thing like you, that's no problem." She scooped Iva effortlessly into strong arms.

The outlines of buildings and houses peeked through the fog after a few minutes, all stone and brick rather than the wooden structures of the cliff-top village. She'd nearly made it all the way to the hamlet before she fell.

"I need to get to Kezik," Iva said.

"Of course, love. Let's take a look at your foot, then we'll get you on the first boat over."

———————◆◆———————

The woman's name was Zefira, and the house she took Iva
to was warm and smelled of fresh-cooked food. Every time
Iva thought she'd counted everyone who lived there, a new
face appeared.

"The kids are yours?" Iva asked as two little girls played
catch with the roll of tape Zefira had used to wrap Iva's
ankle.

"Not mine," Zefira said. "Sisters, nieces, cousins."

"They all live here?"

"Aye. Rest tonight, and we'll go to the docks in the morning."

But Iva, used to living alone except for Lotkia's infre-
quent visits, had trouble resting in this strange house, full
of the sounds of so many people. A strong wind blew in as
the sun set, rattling the windows and clearing the fog away.

Iva dug her telescope out of her bag and hobbled through
the large, labyrinthine house with it tucked under one arm.
The sky was completely clear now, the night air crisp. Trees
full of fragrant white flowers bloomed along the streets,
covering the reek of fish that occasionally drifted up from
the docks. Iva spotted the wandering star within the constellation of the Separated Lovers. She trained her telescope
onto it, and tuned out the sounds around her, focusing on
its quiet song.

"They say it's a bad omen." Iva looked up from the telescope to see Zefira, holding out a sweater.

"It's harmless," Iva said. She took the sweater and
wrapped it around herself. It smelled of sea salt and fresh-
baked bread. "It's a comet. A large ball of ice that loops
around the sun the way the planets do."

"How can you possibly know what it's made of?"

She didn't, really, but the castles of Nor had telescopes vastly more advanced than hers, and Norian children had learned as much about stars and other worlds as they did about their own. She settled for, "My elders told me," and that seemed answer enough for Zefira.

"My elders are more concerned with whether the dishes got done, and whether I'm ever going to marry."

"You're lucky to have them," Iva said solemnly.

"Aye," Zefira agreed.

Iva gestured to the telescope, inviting her to look. Zefira lowered her face to the eyepiece and gasped. "It's a skyfish!"

Iva laughed. "What is a skyfish?"

Zefira shrugged, embarrassed. "That long body, swimming between the stars."

"I suppose it is." Iva looked at the comet as though for the first time, no longer able to concentrate enough to hear its soft song.

⸻ ❈ ⸻

In the morning, Zefira inspected the swollen ankle.

"But I need to get to Kezik," Iva protested when she advised her to stay off of it for a few more days.

"What's so urgent?"

Iva bit her tongue. Honestly, she didn't know if Lotkia was even there. The village was not the only place she traveled with that paraglider.

So she stayed, learning the names of Zefira's many relatives and sharing meals with them. One dish on large half shells looked new and exotic, but the second Iva bit into it, her senses flooded with memory.

"This is Nepo," she said. The familiar taste lingered on her tongue. Zefira offered some other name for it, but Iva shook her head. "It may be that, but on Nor, we called it

'Nepo.'"

"You're Norian?" Zefira's eyes sparked with curiousity. "Is it true you can talk to the waves, change the tides?"

"Some can, but I don't know water songs. I—" She stopped herself before admitting that she heard the songs of stars, worried that might be too strange. "I was young when the island was destroyed."

Iva expected disappointment, but instead, the other woman kept her soft smile and offered Iva another Nepo.

———•◦•———

Once Iva could walk pain-free on her swollen ankle, Zefira took her to the docks to help her negotiate passage across the bay. Iva was surprised at how calm she felt near the water. The cold spray and white soggy sand was very different from the blazing black beaches of Nor, and yet the sound of the slapping waves, the swell and dip of the water's surface was familiar, a friend she hadn't realized she'd been missing.

"Will you stop by when you come back through?" Zefira asked.

She caught the same longing in Zefira's voice that Iva herself had whenever Lotkia left. Indeed, Iva had entertained the idea of staying longer in the hamlet, of staying for good. If her ties to Lotkia were not so strong, if her love had not been so deep, she probably would have.

"I don't know when that will be," Iva said, "But, yes, I will find you again."

It felt unnatural to make such a promise. Iva was the one who stayed put. She was not the wandering star, not the one who came and went like the winds. Only now, she was. Their embrace lingered a little too long. Iva climbed into the boat, turning back to look at Zefira one more time.

The journey across the bay was cold, the train ride through a steep tunnel even colder. It took two days at a slow crawl to ascend all the way to the top of the cliff. Two days without seeing the stars. Two days surrounded by rough stone walls, the low hum of the stone's song almost indistinguishable from the mechanical clang of the funicular.

It was night when the train surfaced at the outskirts of Kezik, and Iva was shocked to see that the comet's tail stretched nearly half the width of the constellation now, and glowed brighter than any of the stars.

She navigated the narrow streets of Kezik on foot, searching for the address she'd only ever seen on an envelope. A chaotic energy pervaded those nighttime streets. Shouting voices echoed off the stone walls. Animals ran free, tearing apart overflowing rubbish bins. Boards covered shop windows, some of them broken or graffitied. Iva knew little about the city except from Lotkia's stories, but none of this seemed normal.

It took all night to find Lotkia's apartment. As sun rays finally sneaked through the city's shadows, Iva knocked. A shuffle came from inside, and the door opened.

She was radiant. Barefoot in a green silk robe that drooped off of one shoulder, dark mess of curls framing her head. Lotkia's hand flew to her mouth in surprise and the corners of eyes crinkled in delight.

"Iva!" She took half a step out the door, glancing over her shoulder. "I wish you'd told me you were coming."

"I wanted—" Iva started, but through the door Lotkia was attempting to block, she saw a man pass by. Dark skin, broad shoulders, and dreadlocks—the firebreather, from the traveling performance troupe back in the village. All the words Iva had rehearsed for this reunion fled her mind.

She turned and fled as well, down the hallway, down the long spiral staircase that descended through the building's heart.

"Iva, wait!" Lotkia yelled. Iva could hardly breathe. She should have known that Lotkia had other lovers. She had known, but in an abstract way that let her believe their love meant more than whatever flings might come and go while they were apart. But that was foolish, she saw now. Wishful thinking. She was only one of those flings as well.

As she kicked open the ground level door, Lotkia caught up and grabbed her arm.

"Iva, wait. I'm glad you're here. I'm so glad you're here. I want to be with you when it happens."

That caught Iva off-guard, and she blinked in confusion. "When what happens?"

Lotkia gave a bewildered shake of her head. "The end of the world, of course."

———————●•●———————

Iva and Sev sat across from each other at Lotkia's kitchen table, an uncomfortable tension between them while Lotkia set newspapers in front of Iva. Iva picked up the papers, holding them high enough to block Sev from her view. Apparently, Kezik scientists had determined the comet was on a direct collision course with the planet. A few days were all they had.

"So it was a bad omen after all," Iva muttered. "Are any of the astronomers Norian?"

Lotkia sat down beside her and wrapped her hands around a steaming mug. She shook her head. "I didn't recognize any." She tapped one of the pages on the table. Iva skimmed but, indeed, there were no names on the list of scientists that looked of Norian origin.

"Then that means no one has asked it not to," Iva said.

"Asked...?" Sev said.

Iva shot him an annoyed look. "I've heard the comet's song."

Lotkia bit her lip, worrying at a chip on the mug with her thumb. "Something so massive would be impossible to move."

"Something so massive," Iva countered, "needs only a small shift to change its course."

<hr>

The three of them went to the edge of the high cliff that evening, away from the chaos and lights of the city. As the sun set, Iva watched the fog blow away from the bay far below, the lights of the fishing hamlet twinkling on at the same rate as the stars overhead.

Lotkia came with her because she knew the songs of the wind, and though she'd never attuned with solar winds before, how different could it be? Sev mainly attuned with fire, but he claimed he heard the songs of water as well, which might help since the comet was mainly ice. Most importantly, all three of them understood that attuning was easier when surrounded by other Norians. Their presence would amplify each other's abilities.

"Listen, about...about Sev," Lotkia said as they walked to the cliff. "When we're apart, you didn't think that..."

Iva glanced over her shoulder at Sev, trailing behind. "No, I didn't. But it hurts to finally see it face to face."

"Why?"

"Why?" Iva shook her head. The question didn't make enough sense to bother with an answer. Instead, she took a deep breath and asked, "Do you love him?"

"Yes," Lotkia answered without hesitation. "Deeply. And

I love you as well. Love is not a finite resource."

Iva was quiet for the rest of the journey. Lotkia's declaration made Iva think of Zefira and her huge family, all the children and elders and everyone in between squeezed into that sprawling house. The way they'd just built on new wings and rooms to fit the family's growth.

By the time they reached the cliff, the comet had risen on the horizon like a second moon. It was so much brighter, so much closer than it had been the night before.

"Skyfish, you grew," Iva whispered.

The three of them sat back-to-back on the rim of the cliff, Iva facing the comet, Sev and Lotkia facing away. Iva started by just listening, which is all she'd ever done before, watching it rise over the horizon until the full, glistening tail became visible. The comet had begun as a small dot between the Separated Lovers, but now it spanned the whole constellation.

After listening for a long time, she began to attune.

The difference between hearing the songs and attuning with them, her father had told her, was the difference between hearing a language and understanding it. You could recognize sounds as words without understanding what those words meant. It had been a metaphor she easily related to, as a refugee child in a strange land, where people were always trying to tell her things she didn't understand.

Several times, the attunement slipped, and if she hadn't had two other Norians there to anchor her, Iva probably couldn't have held it at all. The comet's song recounted its journey through the solar system, the centuries spent in the deep cold of the far away, the tug and pull of celestial bodies, the joyous heating and thawing as it approached the sun, releasing dust and ice to mark its path. Then something shifted. The comet became aware of the attunement, and demanded to know who she was.

Iva tried to convey herself the way the comet had, through the sum of her experiences. The destruction of her island home, her quiet village life, her love for her father, her love for Lotkia. Was the comet listening? Could it possibly understand the song of such a small being on such a different path?

Iva felt the attunement waver; if she was going to make a request, she was running out of time. She asked the comet to change its course, just enough to avoid the pull of this planet's gravity.

"I am Life-Bringer," the comet declared. It reminded her of the booming voice of a Norian priest, echoing off the walls of a cavernous castle.

"There is life here already," Iva told the comet. "If you come here, you will be Death-Bringer."

"I am Life-Bringer," it repeated.

Iva tried to convey the disaster she had lived through, how an ill-intentioned attunement had awoken a dormant volcano and sent ash and lava pouring across the walls of the castles and into the homes of everyone she had ever known. How the sea had steamed and boiled, fish and coral floating charred on the water's surface. How the ground and wind, the water and fire, were all in such turmoil that even the most advanced priests could no longer affect their paths. How she escaped, but so many others did not. She tried to magnify that experience to the size of a comet strike, to multiply her grief from the scale of an island to the scale of a planet.

"You are Life-Bringer," Iva said. "Not Death-Bringer."

She realized she'd spoken that last part out loud. The attunement had broken.

"Did it work?" Lotkia asked. Her back was still pressed

against Iva's.

"I don't know." Iva looked up at the comet, which had nearly crossed the sky by now. More time had passed than she realized—hours that had felt like minutes.

Iva, Lotkia, and Sev made their way to the funicular station, where an all-night tavern served warm stew and cold ale. They were the only ones there, and they ate together in silence. In the cold dawn outside the tavern, Iva listened to the clang and pull of the funicular inside the tunnel, the memory of the taste of Nepo from Zefira's kitchen overpowering the lingering taste of the stew.

Lotkia grasped her hands and pulled her attention away from the abyss.

"Come back to Kezik with me." There was more pleading in her voice than usual, a sincerity that Iva realized had been lacking each time she'd asked before.

"I may," she said. "Someday. But for now, our paths are different."

Lotkia kissed her, and it was just as wonderful as always, and just as painful as always. But this time it was Iva who walked away.

<hr>

The world did not end while Iva rode the train down to the bay, and an unexpected contentment washed over her when she stepped out onto the rocky, foggy shoreline. She negotiated passage across on a fishing boat full of men and women with pierced noses and eyebrows. Life appeared to be going on as usual in the fishing hamlet, with none of the hysteria she'd seen in Kezik.

The wood felt hard beneath her knuckles, the sound of the knock loud in her ears. The time before the door opened stretched to infinity and looped back on itself. Then there she was. Zefira's eyes widened in surprise and her lips stretched into a grin.

"You came back!"

Iva reached for Zefira's hand and raised it to her lips, planting a soft kiss. "I thought I might stay a while. If that's okay with you."

Zefira interlaced her fingers with Iva's and stepped closer. "Stay as long as you want."

The children swarmed out the door and surrounded them, shrieking Iva's name, asking for news from the city. They swept her into the house to show off their latest drawings and inventions.

Later that night, after the fog cleared from the bay, Iva left Zefira sleeping in the bed they'd shared and navigated out of the house so she could go look at the sky. Her telescope stayed packed away, the comet still bright enough to see without it. But it had left the constellation of the Separated Lovers now, and was smaller than the last time she'd seen it. She quieted her mind, focused, and listened to the Skyfish's song as it swam away.

*Sarena Ulibarri is the author of two novellas (*Another Life *from Stelliform Press and* Steel Tree *from Android Press) as well as nearly 50 published short stories. This year, she has sto-*

ries appearing in the anthologies Strange Locations: An Anthology of Dark Travel Guides *(from Apex) and* Solarpunk: Short Stories From Many Futures *(from Flame Tree Press). She is editor-in-chief of World Weaver Press, and a story reviewer and climate fiction editor for Grist Magazine's annual contest Imagine 2200. Find more at www.SarenaUlibarri.com.*

LETTER FROM BAUB AND THE EDITORS

Greetings Boneyard,

As the first issue of *Baubles From Bones* comes to a close, it's hard not to look back at the humble and doe-eyed beginnings of this whacky little zine. From the coffee shop conceptualization meeting, to the exhausting post-work sessions during the holiday season, to reading the hundreds of fantastic stories and poems submitted to us, this zine has gone from being a harebrained idea between a few friends to a real publication led by a team of co-editors and a social media magician, filling the gaps as we go along. And now here you are, holding our first issue. Hold it tightly.

The authors in this issue perfectly encapsulate what we envisioned this zine would be during our initial meetings. They provided a slew of queer, inclusive, thought provoking, and tear jerking stories that we hold near and dear to our hearts. The dancing priestess and queen bring just as much comfort to us as the lonesome alien, feasting beasts, and all the rest. We hope that these stories make as much of an impact on you as they did to us.

From the bottom of our hearts, we would like to say

thank you to our friends and family who have given us nothing but love and support as we embarked upon this wonderful adventure. A very special thanks goes to Jessica Thrower and Greg Clumpner from Parsec for all of the advice and wisdom they generously gave to this fledgling publication. Look forward to the release of their anthology, *Triangulation: Hospitium*, coming later this summer! Thank you to the authors, whose passion, creativity, and trust make this zine possible. Finally, thank you to the readers for taking a chance on this group of sleep deprived goofs, working out of the living room of our apartment. Your support means everything to us.

We can't wait to show you what else we have in store.

From our cozy graveyard to yours,
-Shane, Elyse, and Joel

OUR DONORS

Special thanks to the donors who help support BFB

Gaggle of Ghouls
($1 per month on Patreon or cumulative support of $1-20)

Kylie Barrett

Anonymous

Patricia Enger

Skelly Bellies
($5 per month on Patreon or cumulative support of over $50)

Jayda Troutman

Caroline Ritzert

Anonymous

Zachary Blanner

Ron McNerney

Dylan Zeh

JM Thrower

—◆•◆—

Baubles From Bones is an independently produced and funded publication. It's our passion project! While passion can carry us through late night editing sessions and hours of slush reading, it does not pay writers, cover artists, or the cost of a printing run. That's where regular support through places like Patreon and Ko-fi comes in, helping us keep our graveyard pruned and foggy.

Our supporters get credited in print and on our website, gain access to our Discord server, and receive a copy of each upcoming issue of *Baubles From Bones*.

With additional support, we hope to release audio versions of our stories and raise pay rates for writers and artists.

If you're excited about what we're doing and want to help fund future issues of *BFB*, consider supporting us at patreon.com/baublesfrombones or ko-fi.com/baublesfrombones.